*A
Harlequin
Romance*

OTHER
Harlequin Romances
by MARY BURCHELL

REMEMBERED SERENADE

by

MARY BURCHELL

HARLEQUIN BOOKS   TORONTO
WINNIPEG

Original hard cover edition published in 1975
by Mills & Boon Limited

SBN 373-01936-X

Harlequin edition published December 1975

Printed in Canada

1936

CHAPTER ONE

'DARLING! It would be your first star role!' Mrs. Ransome clasped her hands together and gazed in satisfaction at her daughter.

'No, Mother, not exactly.' Joanna instinctively adopted the commonsense tone which she used when her mother became intense. 'It's little more than a performance by advanced students, you know.'

'But in public. And yours is the principal role.'

'The principal female role,' Joanna corrected.

'Well – there you are!' Mrs. Ransome put a low value on mere male singers, unless of course they were very handsomely costumed and made a good foil for the leading soprano.

'The tenor is very important in this work,' Joanna stated firmly. 'And the bass role is terrific, both musically and dramatically. That's why they're bringing in Peter Ellsworthy for the occasion.'

'Who is he?' Her mother's tone reduced the gentleman to chorus level.

'Oh, Mother! He has done any amount of very distinguished work. He's even sung quite important roles at the Garden. I'm thrilled at the thought of singing with him. We have a tremendous scene together. He strangles me.' She smiled happily at this pleasing prospect.

'*Strangles* you? I don't call that very nice!'

'It isn't meant to be nice,' Joanna explained patiently. 'You see – well, never mind. You'll have plenty of time to study the libretto between now and the performance. I won't give you a résumé of the plot now. And of course you understand I'm in the second cast. Martha Singleton has the first night.'

'Why?' asked Mrs. Ransome disapprovingly.

'Because she has a better voice than I have,' replied Joanna honestly.

'I don't believe it!' Her mother bridled indignantly.

'Oh, but she has! It's quite splendid. She'll be a real dramatic soprano one day. She doesn't sing quite as well as I do, though,' Joanna added, without either conceit or false modesty. 'And I have the edge over her when it comes to acting. In fact, I think I got the part more on my acting than my singing.'

'What did you say the work was called?'

' "The Love of Three Kings".'

'I don't think I've ever heard of it.'

'It isn't very often done. It was written about – oh, I don't know – 1912 or 1913, I think, by a man called Montemezzi. Some very famous people did it in their time – Emilia Trangoni among others. It was her last role before she died.'

'You mean it's usually done by an *old* woman?'

'No, no! It's a young woman's part. Trangoni was the one who was killed in a riding accident on her thirtieth birthday, you know. You would have been a girl at the time.'

'I think I do remember the name.' Mrs. Ransome wrinkled her forehead thoughtfully. 'Is it a long opera?'

'Three acts. But the soprano is killed at the end of the second act.'

'What a stupid idea! No wonder it isn't a very well known opera,' said Mrs. Ransome scornfully.

'You may have something there,' Joanna agreed with a laugh. And, not for the first time, she was impressed by the way her silly – though very sweet – mother could stumble on a profound truth.

There was an easy-going and charming relationship between the two. Joanna, who could hardly remember her father, had adopted a slightly maternal attitude towards her mother for more years than she could measure. There had always been something appealing and helpless about Mrs. Ransome, although, like a lot of fragile-looking women, she had a strain of toughness which disagreeably surprised anyone who came up against her most treasured convictions. The strongest of these convictions was that her one child was distinctly more remarkable than anyone else's child.

This attitude, which might well have spoiled a less well-balanced girl, amused and rather touched Joanna. From time to time she brought her mother up short, in the nicest possible way, and forced her to accept a slightly more reasonable view of things. But inevitably Mrs. Ransome slipped back into her favourite little bits of self-delusion, from which she derived a good deal of fairly harmless contentment.

Life had not been too kind to her, and Joanna was aware of this. The husband she adored – and on whom she had willingly relied for most decisions and the tackling of most difficulties – had died suddenly of a heart attack when Joanna was only seven years old. After everything had been settled up and a not unimpressive life insurance policy gathered in, Mrs. Ransome found herself in possession of a pleasant, quite well-appointed house, and a very modest income.

Her vigorous and capable sister-in-law had made various suggestions about the ways in which she could augment this income. But Mrs. Ransome had blenched at the thought of pursuing any of these. The role of pretty, slightly helpless widow became her admirably, and this she played with moderate success throughout Joanna's schooldays and into her years as a singing student.

Joanna's Aunt Georgina thought – and indeed said, because she believed in giving her opinions, sought or unsought – that music in general and singing in particular hardly promised a secure future, and added that Joanna would do better to train for something less what she called 'airy-fairy'. But Joanna, who believed in her own gifts, was easily persuaded by her mother at least to take the chance of seeing how far her talent would take her.

'It isn't as though we can't afford it, provided we're careful about other things,' her mother insisted. 'And your Aunt Georgina doesn't know everything, even if she thinks she does.'

Nevertheless, Mrs. Ransome was sufficiently in awe of her sister-in-law to attach a good deal of value to her approval. After all, she was a highly successful head-mistress, though now retired. And so Mrs. Ransome now remarked with a good deal of satisfaction, 'Even Georgina should be impressed by your being cast for such a role.'

Joanna looked sceptical. In her experience Aunt Georgina took a good deal of impressing. But she knew nothing would stop her mother doing some harmless boasting about her, so she said no more.

The very next day, when she came in from the music college she attended each day, she realized from the slightly raised voices issuing from the sitting-room that her aunt had called and that her mother was already in

8

full flight.

'It's a most unusual opera – very rarely done,' she heard her mother say. 'Very gratifying for Joanna to be chosen.'

'What is the name of this unusual opera?' her aunt's voice inquired briskly.

'Something about the "Love of Three – of Three—" '

' "The Love of Three Oranges",' said Aunt Georgina knowledgeably. 'By Prokofiev.'

'No, that wasn't the name,' Joanna heard her mother say doubtfully. 'It's by someone called Montezuma or something like that.'

'Most improbable,' stated Aunt Georgina with authority. 'Montezuma was an Aztec Emperor in the sixteenth century.'

'O-oh—' Poor Mrs. Ransome sounded so flummoxed that Joanna came to the rescue.

'It's "The Love of Three Kings", Aunt Georgina,' she said, coming into the room. 'And it's by Montemezzi.'

'I've never heard of it,' stated Aunt Georgina, as though this automatically down-rated its artistic value.

'*Haven't* you?' Mrs. Ransome seized the advantage. 'Quite a lot of famous people have sung in it. Including one very famous one who died on her thirtieth birthday, poor thing. Isn't that sad?' she added quite inconsequentially.

'Not necessarily,' replied her sister-in-law. 'I've heard some singers I would have regarded as expendable long before their thirtieth birthdays.'

'Georgina, that isn't a very kind thing to say!' exclaimed Mrs. Ransome reproachfully.

9

'It was not intended to be kind,' retorted Miss Ransome, who had enjoyed a reputation for a somewhat caustic wit throughout her school career. A reputation which had no effect, however, on her capacity to turn out pupils who were very reasonably well behaved and quite astonishingly well educated. Indeed, it is even possible that there was some connection between the two things.

'I suppose,' she went on, 'you are referring to Emilia Trangoni.'

'Yes, that's right!' Joanna smiled at her aunt. 'You do have a tremendous fund of general knowledge, Aunt Georgina, don't you? I mean, Trangoni's was not exactly a world-famous name, I imagine.'

'I have a useful smattering of knowledge on a variety of subjects,' her aunt conceded with some satisfaction. 'But then I was fortunate enough to be born before the passion for educational specialization. Today people are regarded with awe if they know a good deal about two largely useless subjects, even if they are grossly ignorant about their own incomparable language.'

This, of course, is the kind of statement which, unhappily true though it may be, is calculated to bring most conversations to a full stop. There was therefore a pause. Then Aunt Georgina took up the subject again herself.

'Tragoni,' she repeated thoughtfully. 'Old Justin Wilmore should have something about her in that collection of his. If she was famous in this unusual role he would be sure to have photographs and programmes, possibly even costumes.'

'Aunt Georgina! what a wonderful idea!' A streak of excited colour showed on Joanna's high cheekbones, and her grey eyes widened and sparkled. 'Do you think perhaps I could—'

'Who is Justin Wilmore?' inquired Mrs. Ransome, slightly out of her depth once more.

'He lives in that attractive greystone house about a mile from my new bungalow,' her sister-in-law explained briefly. 'Something of a recluse, of course, though he was very courteous when I stopped to admire his roses the other day. A little vague in his manner, but a gentleman. Unquestionably a gentleman.'

'But how could he help Joanna?' Mrs. Ransome's mind was one-track when it came to her daughter's interests.

'He has a famous collection of operatic scores and photographs and costumes – that sort of thing,' Joanna explained. 'Aunt Georgina is right. He might well have something on *my* role. The only question is – how do I get to see him?'

'I shall give you an introduction,' her aunt stated.

'On the strength of a chat about roses?' Mrs. Ransome sounded rather disparaging.

'We spoke of other things besides roses,' replied Aunt Georgina, which naturally raised such interesting possibilities in her sister-in-law's mind that her beautiful soft dark eyes took on an unnecessarily speculative expression.

'Don't be silly, Pansy,' said Aunt Georgina. (Mrs. Ransome really was called Pansy, and astonishingly well the name suited her, somehow.) 'I shall open negotiations, Joanna,' Aunt Georgina went on magisterially. 'And when—' she did not say 'if', Joanna noticed – 'when I have arranged an interview for you, I shall telephone and you can come down. It will give you an opportunity to see my new bungalow at the same time.'

'I should love that, Aunt Georgina,' Joanna said sincerely. 'And I can't thank you enough.'

'Thank me when the interview has been arranged,' replied her aunt. And then she took her leave.

'Georgina *means* well, of course,' said Mrs. Ransome somewhat elliptically when they were alone.

'Indeed she does!' agreed Joanna, who was feeling very well disposed towards her aunt at the moment. 'And she almost always manages to carry out whatever she decides to do. It couldn't be more fortunate, Mother! If she really gets me an opportunity to see the Wilmore collection and talk to the old gentleman himself, it will be a tremendous help. Provided he has anything on this particular work, I mean. It's invaluable to get a good rich background of information when one is studying a character like this. I shall enjoy seeing Aunt G's new bungalow too. I wish she'd suggested your coming with me.'

'I don't,' replied Mrs. Ransome without rancour. 'You would naturally go on your own to see this Mr. Wilmore, and I should be left with Georgina. And although I'm very fond of her, of course—' she paused, as though reviewing this statement and finding it not quite accurate — 'I do find her manner rather *wearing* at times. Anyway, I suppose you'll only be away for the day.'

In this she was wrong, however. Georgina Ransome did nothing by halves. A week later Joanna received a letter written in her aunt's strong, legible hand.

'My dear Joanna, Your telephone appears to be out of order. Or else you and your mother have been out a great deal. Anyway, the interview with Mr.

12

Wilmore is arranged. He will expect you at his house at 2.30 next Saturday afternoon. I suggest you catch the 10.30 Green Line bus from Victoria to Dalrymple Corner. This is a *request* stop, so be on the lookout for it soon after the bus leaves Pethwick Green. It should arrive at the Corner at 12.2 but is frequently late. When you get out walk about three hundred yards *in the same direction as the bus*, and you will see my bungalow on the right-hand side.

'I shall give you lunch, of course, and then drive you to the gate of Mr. Wilmore's house. I should like you to stay the night with me afterwards, as I shall want to hear a full account of what happens. The Sunday bus service back is quite a good one. There is a convenient bus at 9.45 a.m. – Your affectionate Aunt Georgina.'

'Why does she give you the sort of directions one would give to a child?' said Joanna's mother rather crossly. 'Doesn't she realize you're a responsible adult by now?'

'It doesn't matter.' Joanna smiled happily. 'She's actually arranged it, bless her heart! It's a chance in a thousand.'

Intensely musical though she was, Joanna had always had as much interest in the drama of what she was singing, which was probably why opera had always appealed to her more than concert work. On a stage – even no more than the stage at the college – she immediately felt involved in a character, not from a merely superficial point of view but in real depth. She liked to study the background, the origins of the person she was to perform, and she was passionately interested to hear of any famous exponent of a role. To browse through the Wilmore collection was going to be an experience after her own heart. And the fact that she was to stay with her aunt for the night afterwards was not irksome to her, as it would have been to her mother.

Joanna was genuinely fond of her rather formidable Aunt Georgina and, unlike her mother, guessed that self-sufficient though she might seem, Aunt Georgina was often lonely – missing the girls who had made up so much of her active life. If it would please her to have her niece stay with her and discuss hopes and plans for the future, then Joanna was more than ready to afford her that minor pleasure in return for the very real service her aunt was doing her.

It was a beautiful early autumn morning when Joanna set out, the kind of morning to lift the heart and encourage bright hopes. And the drive out of London to the quite unspoiled part of Sussex where Aunt Georgina now lived was a rare pleasure to Joanna. She loved her life in London, and revelled in the musical world in which she worked and lived; but the sight of golden cornfields and green pastureland soothed and charmed her, and put her in a hopeful mood for her interview with Justin Wilmore.

She wondered what he would be like. 'A gentleman,' Aunt Georgina had said. And, from the one or two details she had added, Joanna guessed a gentleman in the rather old-world sense of the word. Well, that was something she could appreciate and enjoy. If they were to talk of bygone days and great performances of the past, no brash or harsh note should be allowed to creep in.

She gazed out of the window at the passing landscape, and presently the peace and tranquillity of the scene began to merge with her own thoughts. She contentedly imagined herself gathering so much valuable information about the heroine of 'The Love of Three Kings' that when she finally came to perform the part the critics would say something like: 'Joanna Ransome not only sang the part of Fiora admirably but gave an impersonation of the character which was remarkable in one so young and inexperienced. It was as though she had penetrated to the innermost thoughts of the tragic princess—'

'Pethwick Green,' called out the driver, jerking her out of her happy day-dream into the realization that she was nearing her destination. She asked the driver to stop at the next request stop and sat looking out for Dalrymple Corner. It gave her a certain amount of pleasure to notice that her watch registered exactly two minutes past twelve as the bus came to a halt.

She was the only passenger to descend at this point, and the driver gave her a friendly wave as he drove on. She stood there for a moment or two, taking in the full charm of the scene, telling herself, 'Perhaps I shall remember this all my life as the place from which I started off to the interview that launched me on my real career.'

She laughed a little at the fanciful notion, though she felt more than half serious about it. Then, still in a pleasant half-dream, she went to cross the country road. As she did so, a bright green sports car came swooping round the corner at considerable speed. With an exclamation of alarm Joanna jumped back on to the grass verge, missed her footing and fell backwards into the ditch at the side of the road.

She heard the car skid to a standstill and, as she began to pick herself out of a nasty mixture of mud and nettles, the driver came running up – to apologize, as she fondly imagined. Before she could start to reassure him, however, he addressed her in tones of the utmost irritation.

'And what do you think *you* were doing? Trying to commit suicide?'

'No. Trying to avoid some idiot who was driving much too fast,' retorted Joanna, aware that she was not appearing to advantage on her hands and knees and covered with dust.

'If you don't mind my saying so—'

'I do mind your saying so – if you're proposing to blame me for your own irresponsible driving,' she interrupted. 'And instead of berating me, you might help me out of this ditch!'

'I'm sorry,' he said stiffly and, extending a strong looking brown hand, he hauled her out of the ditch with some dexterity and began to brush her down.

'I can see to that myself, thank you.' She spoke stiffly in her turn.

'You're not hurt, are you?' He sounded slightly more concerned now, possibly because he was beginning to recover from his own fright.

'No. Except for some nettle stings and a shaking.'

'I'm sorry,' he said again. 'Can I drive you anywhere?'

'No, thank you. I'm only walking a little way along the road.'

'Well then—' he hesitated.

'Don't let me keep you.' She was not even looking at him as she brushed some dust from the sleeve of her best suit. 'I'm quite all right.'

'Very well.' He turned and went towards his car. Then suddenly he retraced his steps and, looking up, she really saw him for the first time, taking in the fact that he was big and broad-shouldered and that his thick brown hair had more than a touch of red in it. She also noticed that all the anger seemed to have faded from his face and that his dark eyes were looking at her in a slightly shamed way.

'Look here, I'm *really* sorry—'

'I believe you, for it's the third time you've said so,' she told him, and she laughed suddenly and felt her annoyance evaporate.

'It was my fault,' he admitted reluctantly. 'I *was* driving too fast. And I was thinking hard about something that was worrying me, which is an idiotic thing to do when you're driving.'

'Well, *I* was thinking hard about something too,' she confessed. 'Only with me it was something nice and exciting. I expect it was half my own fault. I just walked out into the road without a thought of traffic, which is equally idiotic.'

'Then we're quits?' He held out his hand and smiled in a quick, infectious way. 'I hope whatever you're excited about turns out to be as nice as you expect.'

'And I,' said Joanna, putting her hand into his, 'hope you don't really need to be worrying, after all — that everything comes right, in fact.'

'I expect it will.' He was still smiling as he released her hand. 'I just have to keep an eye on a nice elderly uncle of mine who's never learned to look after himself. People are always imposing on him, and I'm just making sure it doesn't happen again.'

With a friendly wave of his hand, he went back to his car and drove off, while Joanna looked after him thoughtfully and said, 'Oh—?' She watched him drive away and then walked on towards Aunt Georgina's bungalow, telling herself that there must be lots of nice elderly uncles about, and there was no reason to suppose—

Aunt Georgina welcomed her cordially, though she seemed to think Joanna's explanation for her dusty condition unsatisfactory.

'How could you fall into a ditch?' she wanted to know. 'I never heard of anything so silly, just because a car frightened you.'

'I suppose it was rather silly,' Joanna admitted, as she sponged the last mud-spots from her skirt. 'Aunt Georgina, has Mr. Wilmore got a nephew?'

'Not to my knowledge. Why?'

'Oh, nothing. I'm rather glad to hear he hasn't, that's all.'

And to Aunt Georgina's credit, she pressed the matter no further, knowing from long, long experience that girls asked very odd questions at times; and when they then claimed that the question meant 'nothing' they were really saying that they didn't want to be asked any questions in their turn.

She gave Joanna an excellent lunch, and then got out her battered little Mini and drove her to the gate of Wilmore Manor, a tall, exceptionally beautiful wrought-iron affair, through which Joanna could already see the roses which had attracted her aunt's congratulations, and a pleasant grey-stone house with white-painted shutters.

'Now you are on your own,' Aunt Georgina said to her niece as she got out of the car. 'Good luck, and don't muff your chances.'

Joanna was too excited by now to do more than murmur some indistinct reply. Then she pushed open the tall gate and, having closed it again carefully behind her, she walked up the short drive to the house. A timid tug at the polished brass bell-pull produced a musical sound somewhere in the back regions of the house, and almost immediately a somewhat elderly manservant opened the door to her.

She explained rather breathlessly who she was and he admitted her, observing that Mr. Wilmore was expecting her, and would she please follow him?

He led the way along a thickly carpeted corridor to a half-open door. Voices in the room indicated that Mr. Wilmore was not alone and, as the servant put out his hand to open the door further, a disagreeably familiar voice said, in answer to some murmured objection,

'I don't care what you say, I'm willing to bet she's just another clever young cadger. Whoever heard of her, anyway? She's nothing but a student, apparently, and quite unworthy of—'

'Miss Ransome,' announced the manservant respectfully. Then he stood aside for Joanna to enter the room.

This she did, in as good order as she could, considering what she had just overheard. A tall, grey-haired man rose from a chair and came across to greet her with an air of great politeness, while she was not at all surprised to see that the other occupant of the room was the young man who – as she now angrily phrased it to herself – had pushed her into the ditch.

'Miss Ransome—' Mr. Wilmore took her hand in his long, thin one – 'how kind of you to be so punctual. Your aunt told me you would be coming all the way from London. You must have made an early start.'

'Not really.' Joanna smiled at him, and liked him on sight. 'And anyway, it's you who are being so kind as to allow me to come and see you. Believe me, I do appreciate the privilege.'

'Not at all.' His pleasant, rather short-sighted eyes surveyed her with some pleasure. Then, as though recollecting something, he included the other man in the conversation. 'This is my nephew, Elliot Cheam. You've probably heard of him.'

'The theatrical producer?' Joanna was startled into exclaiming.

'Yes. Have you met each other before?'

'Briefly,' said the young man before Joanna could either claim or repudiate the honour. 'In fact, I almost ran Miss Ransome down a couple of hours ago. Accidentally, of course,' he added in a tone which somehow conveyed that he would have been partially justified if he had done it on purpose.

'You were not hurt, I hope?' Mr. Wilmore looked quite anxiously at his young guest.

'Oh, no! In London we get used to skipping out of the way of badly driven cars,' declared Joanna with a charming little laugh.

'Well—' her host looked faintly surprised – 'we have quite a lot to discuss, I believe. So we won't keep you, Elliot, if you want to go over to see Sara. Give her my best wishes.'

'I thought perhaps of going this evening—' his nephew began. But the older man spoke with courteous authority.

'This afternoon would be better,' he stated, in the nicest way possible. 'I should like to talk with Miss Ransome on her own.'

For an incredible moment Joanna had a childish impulse to put out her tongue at Elliot Cheam. She resisted this, of course, but was somewhat taken aback to find that anything so juvenile could even occur to her.

'Now—' when the nephew had left, with a not altogether good grace and the merest nod in Joanna's direction, Justin Wilmore indicated two comfortable chairs in one of the pleasant window bays — 'you must tell me what it is that specially interests you. My collection is a pretty big one – for a private collector, that is. But although my nephew thinks I am not a very well organized person—' his eyes twinkled a little – 'I can usually put my hand on anything special.'

'I must explain first that I'm not really much more than an advanced student,' said Joanna, determined that no one should be able to hold it against her that she exaggerated her importance. 'At the music college where I'm training we're going to do Montemezzi's opera "The Love of Three Kings"—'

'Oh? "L'Amore dei Tre Re"?' Her host smiled immediately. 'A very beautiful work.'

'You've heard it done?'

'Certainly. Several times. It was done more often in my youth than nowadays. The most beautiful Fiora was—'

'Emilia Trangoni,' said Joanna quickly. 'Isn't that right? Did you actually hear her?'

'Oh, yes. She was unforgettable in the part,' Justin Wilmore said quietly. 'In an odd way, you remind me a little of her.'

'*Do* I?' Joanna was pleased and flattered beyond measure. 'In what way?'

'Partly the shape of the face, I suppose. And you are much the same build. Besides—' the faintly reflective smile suggested that he was delving back into the past with a rare nostalgic pleasure – 'there is the same quality of what I can only call questing innocence, if you don't mind my being somewhat personal.'

'I don't mind a bit. I'm flattered and charmed.' Joanna declared sincerely. 'But how – how very perceptive of you to recognize such a subtle quality. And to have remembered it from another singer so long ago.'

'Oh, one does remember these things,' her host assured her, still with that reflective smile. 'One sees them so seldom, and one should never forget them. The moment you mentioned the part of Fiora I realized why it was you reminded me of Emilia – of Trangoni. It is a quality that belongs essentially to Fiora too, that questing innocence. She is intensely innocent, although she commits a sin. That is the essence of her. – But I am interrupting you. You were saying that there is to be a performance of this work at your music college.'

'You were not interrupting me, really,' Joanna assured him eagerly. 'You were talking exactly as I hoped you would talk. You see, I'm to sing Fiora, and I want desperately to get the full measure of the part – to understand the character in depth. Anything you can tell me about the role – or the singers who did the part in other days – would fascinate me and help me. And if you have anything in the way of photographs or reviews—'

'I have them all,' he said musingly. 'All that related to Trangoni, that is. And photographs of some of the other famous exponents of the part. It is, as you probably know, the kind of role that can be sung by a dramatic soprano or a lyric. Ponselle, Muzio, Bori – they all sang it in their time.'

'And you heard them all?' Joanna caught her breath.

'In my youth – yes.'

'But Trangoni was your favourite?'

'She came a little later in my life.' Again that thoughtful smile, as though an old film were unrolling before his charmed vision. 'She had not the magnificent voice of any of those three, I suppose. But the difference was that I was in love with her.'

'You were?' Insensibly, Joanna's voice softened. 'How – how good of you to tell me. It somehow brings her quite near, when you talk of her like that. She died very tragically, didn't she?'

'Yes. She was killed in a riding accident on her thirtieth birthday. Just beyond that row of trees.' He pointed out of the window to a glade of trees that covered a nearby hill.

'You mean – *here?* in this very district?' Joanna felt her throat tighten with excitement and pity.

'Yes. They brought her here. She died an hour later in this room.'

'Mr. Wilmore! I'm most terribly sorry. I – I had no idea that I was arousing such memories. It's – it's like intruding into your private affairs. I didn't mean—'

'Don't apologize, my dear.' He put out his hand and touched hers reassuringly. 'Do you suppose I don't like to talk about her? It was all of thirty-five years ago, and I'm an old man now. Old people like to retrace their most cherished memories, you know. In some indefinable way, you recalled her as soon as you came into the room. To talk about her to you seems quite – logical. I hope you don't find it at all embarrassing.'

Joanna shook her read and swallowed a slight lump in her throat.

'On the contrary. It's – it's a sort of rare privilege to hear you talk like this. Could you tell me a little of how you remember her in the role of Fiora?'

'Of course. But first *you* must tell *me* how you see the part. One should never superimpose one interpretation on another.'

'Well, she – as you said, in a way she is essentially innocent, isn't she? She has been forced into marriage while she loved someone else, and so she feels justified in still meeting her lover, although her conscience troubles her.'

'She is innocent, though her conscience troubles her,' he agreed. 'I supoose that is the basic driving force behind her actions. And how about her relationship with the old man – her father-in-law?'

'Oh, she's afraid of him. Deathly afraid!' Joanna actually shuddered slightly. 'Because he *knows*, doesn't he?'

'No, he suspects. But because he is blind he cannot absolutely confirm his suspicions. And in his way he loves her.'

'As a man?' asked Joanna quickly.

'Possibly. He has been a great, vigorous, successful warrior in his day, remember. He is jealous on behalf of his son, but possibly on his own behalf too. Some play it one way, some another. Pinza was the greatest I ever saw in the part. He gave the most terrifying impression of being jealous *of* his own son as well as *for* him. It is in this tremendous conflict of feeling that he finally strangles her.'

'Yes,' Joanna said, 'Yes, I see. You make it all so *real*. What was Trangoni's greatest moment?'

'Oddly enough, at a point when she was not singing, lovely though her voice was. You remember when her blind father-in-law finds her on the battlements at night, and she manages to give a fairly satisfactory reason for being there. He is not entirely convinced and, taking her face in his hands, he *feels* all over it trying to decide if she is innocent or not. In those moments Trangoni gave the impression that every inch of her flesh crawled with terror and guilt, and yet she managed to look like an innocent girl. Great acting — great acting.'

'Then she was a very fine actress too?'

'Yes. Perhaps a finer actress than singer. I don't know. She never reached her full development vocally. And anyway, I am not an unprejudiced judge.' He smiled that very charming smile again, and Joanna thought how good-looking he must have been thrity-five years ago. Much better looking than that horrid, aggressive nephew of his, she thought in passing. Then she dismissed Elliot Cheam from her thoughts again. He fitted nowhere into this romantic, touching story of the past.

'Would you like to see something in the way of photographs and costumes now?' her host asked.

'You have her costumes too?' breathed Joanna in awe.

'Yes, many of them. Certainly her Fiora costumes. Come with me and I'll show you.'

She followed him in something of a daze, through the house and into a large, light annexe which had obviously been built on to the house at a much later date than the original building. Here, ranged in drawers and cupboards, there were scores and programmes and photographs, all meticulously catalogued. He opened a few and displayed to her some of the treasures of his collection, and then took down what was obviously one of his very special folders.

'Here are the first-night programmes of everything Trangoni ever sang,' he explained, and it struck Joanna that the collection was pitifully small – the highlights of a short, short career. Reverently she turned the leaves, catching sight of magical names like La Scala, Covent Garden, Teatro Reale Roma. Then, as she silently returned the folder to him, he took down a photograph and gave it into her hands.

It is rather rarely that one can see a likeness to oneself in another person. But as Joanna stared down at the half smiling girl who looked back at her, she said impulsively. 'I see what you mean! She is a little like me. Except that she looks a personality and I don't,' she added honestly.

'Not yet, perhaps. But you will.' Justin Wilmore looked amused. 'And of course her eyes were darker than yours.'

'Mine aren't dark at all,' Joanna said exactly. 'They're grey.'

'But the lashes are very dark,' he replied without even looking at her, so that she had the extraordinary conviction that he already carried an accurate impression of her in his mind. 'Here are one or two other photographs of her in various roles. As Mimi – she was a charming Mimi – and as Nedda. And here is one of her as Desdemona. And – let me see – yes, here is the photograph of her as Fiora.'

'Oh! That's just as Fiora should look,' exclaimed Joanna delightedly. 'I see what you mean! I see what you mean. And what a gorgeous costume. And the way her hair is caught in that jewellel net. It's lovely!'

'Would you like to see the costume?' He put down the file of photographs and led the way to a large press at the end of the room, and when he flung open the double doors Joanna gasped. Her delighted gaze rested on one glorious stage costume after another, while

26

ranged on shelves at the side were costume jewellery, belts, shoes, fans and all the essential additions which make up an arresting whole on a stage.

Justin Wilmore lifted down a graceful dress, with a slight swirling train, which hung a little limply from the hanger as though crying out for a young, girlish figure on which to display itself. The dress shaded from pale flesh-pink at the close neckline to almost blood-coloured beads on the train.

'It's wonderful!' Joanna touched it with awed fingers.

'And here is the jewelled hairnet she wore.' With his disengaged hand he reached to the back of one of the shelves, took out a pearl-studded net and put it into Joanna's hands.

In that second she had the most extraordinary feeling that she all but touched the soft hair of the girl who had once worn it.

'Do you want to try it on?' asked her host at that moment.

'*Try it on?* Oh, I – I couldn't. It would be sacrilege even to put it on one's hair.'

'I didn't mean only the net. Would you like to try on the whole costume? I can't imagine anything that would give you, literally, more the "feel" of the part, as the saying is.'

'Mr. Wilmore, you can't mean it?' Awe and excited temptation struggled in Joanna's heart. 'It's so – precious. To you personally as well as for its own intrinsic worth.'

'That's why I should like to see you in it. She wore it only once. I should like to see her – you – in it again. Come, I'll call my housekeeper and she'll look after you.'

And, lightly throwing the costume over his arm, he went rapidly towards the door, with Joanna following behind, holding the jewelled net as though it were gold dust.

'Mrs, Trimble—' he called to someone who was passing at the far end of the hall – 'you're just the person I want. Have you a few minutes to look after my young friend, Miss Ransome? She has come to see me about an operatic performance in which she is taking part; and I should like to see her in this costume.'

'That costume?' Mrs. Trimble had approached during this speech and now stood gazing at the dress with astonished eyes. '*That costume?*' she repeated, and she could not have sounded more shocked if her employer had proposed to wrap Joanna in the altar-cloth of St. Paul's Cathedral. 'But it's – it's—'

'Yes, I know it is,' agreed Mr. Wilmore good-humouredly. 'But Miss Ransom is to play this particular role – and there's a sort of likeness – and anyway, I want to see her in the costume,' he finished on the peremptory note of a man who hardly knows how to explain his own impulse.

'Very well, sir,' said Mrs. Trimble and, taking the dress carefully over her arm, she led the way upstairs, Joanna following, still holding the jewelled net.

Having conducted Joanna to a charming bedroom overlooking the front of the house, the housekeeper turned to her and said with an air of respectful but irrepressible curiosity, 'Excuse my asking, miss, but are you a relative or a family friend?'

'I'm neither, Mrs. Trimble,' replied Joanna frankly. 'And you're no more astonished than I am. I never met Mr. Wilmore before today, and I understand this costume is among his most treasured possessions. The suggestion that I should try it on certainly didn't come from me. In fact, I feel rather awful about it. Except—' she glanced longingly at the costume which now was spread out on the bed.

'Well, any girl would want to wear it, I suppose,' the housekeeper conceded with a smile, for Joanna's candour evidently met with her approval. 'It's just that I've never known Mr. Wilmore to allow anyone even to touch that particular dress before. Sometimes his friends from the musical world come here, you know, but only to *look* at things, or check up something in a score. I certainly don't ever remember anyone trying on a – a Trangoni costume.'

'Do a lot of musical people come here?' inquired Joanna, as she slipped off her jacket and skirt.

'Mostly Mr. Wilmore's personal friends. People like Mr. Warrender, the conductor – though I suppose we should call him Sir Oscar now he's been knighted. And of course Lady Warrender comes too. She's Anthea Benton, the singer, you know. She tried on one or two of the costumes once. But not any of the Trangoni ones. I noticed Mr. Wilmore said something about there being a likeness—' she looked consideringly at Joanna. 'I see what he means. You've somehow a look of *her*. She died young, and—'

'I know. He told me,' Joanna said gently.

'He did?' Mrs. Trimble looked as though wonders would never cease, as she herself would have put it. 'Well, I suppose he knows what he wants—' She broke off and looked from the window as there came the sound of a car driving up to the front of the house. 'Why, here's Mr. Elliot back again already. And Miss Sara with him,' she added, with a subtle change in her tone which somehow suggested to Joanna that 'Miss

29

Sara' was not among her favourite people.

'Oh, dear!' The vexed exclamation slipped out before Joanna could prevent it, for the last thing she wanted was to have Elliot Cheam, of all people, see her parading in one of his uncle's famous costumes. If she read him aright, he was bound to draw all the wrong conclusions.

She became aware that the housekeeper was looking at her with some surprise and, in order to divert attention from her impulsive exclamation, she asked quickly, 'Did you ever see Emilia Trangoni, Mrs. Trimble?'

'Oh, yes. She came here often in the last year of her life, and I'd already been housekeeper then for four or five years. She was a lovely lady, and she was going to marry Mr. Wilmore. It was all very sad. Do you want any help with your hairdressing, Miss Ransome? I think I can remember just the way she wore it, with the ends caught up in that little net at the back.'

So Joanna willingly submitted to the housekeeper's ministrations, and literally held her breath when the beautiful stage costume was lifted carefully over her head and allowed to fall in graceful folds around her slim figure.

'You look beautiful,' said Mrs. Trimble simply. 'And — yes, I do see what Mr. Wilmore means. You look extraordinarily like — her in that dress. It was designed specially for her, of course.'

'At least I don't look at all like myself.' Joanna surveyed herself in the long mirror and it seemed to her that another girl looked back at her. 'It's almost uncanny,' she exclaimed, catching her breath on a little gasp.

'Well, one doesn't need to be too fanciful about these

things,' declared Mrs. Trimble briskly. 'A stage dress always changes anyone a good deal. After all, it has been deliberately designed to give the impression of a special person. Are you ready to go down now? I expect Mr. Wilmore is waiting. Be careful of the train. It's easy to trip if you're not used to wearing a period costume like that.'

'I'll be careful,' Joanna promised as she preceded the housekeeper out of the room and started towards the head of the stairs. As she did so she heard Elliot Cheam's voice in the hall, as though he were speaking over his shoulder to someone in the drawing-room, and a few moments later he came bounding up the stairs, two steps at a time.

They met almost head on at the top of the flight, and he stopped dead, his colour actually fading in a wave of anger far exceeding anything he had shown over the incident with the car.

'What the – hell do you think you're doing?' For the second time that day he was querying her behaviour, but this time his tone implied that an unforgivable offence had been committed. 'Take off that dress at once!' His voice actually shook with fury. 'It's one of my uncle's most treasured—'

'Mr. Wilmore wanted Miss Ransome to try it on, sir,' stated Mrs. Trimble primly in the background.

'Wanted her to—?'

'You don't suppose I would be wearing this dress without his permission, do you?' Joanna's eyes flashed with anger as she stared defiantly back at him. 'He asked me—'

'He *asked* you?' The contempt in his tone was like a blow in the face. 'I suppose you mean that you some-how persuaded him into agreeing.'

'I did nothing of the kind! The offer – the suggestion – was entirely his.'

'You don't say!' He laughed angrily, though he stepped back to allow her to proceed. But as she passed him he said in a voice too low for the housekeeper to hear, 'You are a fast worker, aren't you?'

She longed to make some crushing retort – to justify herself in the face of that scornful, sceptical smile – but no words would come. Instead, she started on her way down the stairs, trembling with anger and an absurd sense of guilt, generated entirely by Elliot Cheam's attitude.

'But I've no reason to feel guilty!' she told herself. 'No reason at all. I'm completely innocent, whatever he likes to imply. I wish I'd never put on the dress now, but I'm quite justified—'

And then she saw Justin Wilmore cross the hall and come to stand at the foot of the stairs. He leaned his arm on the end of the curving bannister and stared up at her.

'Emilia!' he said in a half whisper. And he looked at Joanna as though she were a ghost, walking towards him out of his long-lost youth.

CHAPTER TWO

For a moment the spell was complete. Then Joanna came down the rest of the stairs and smiled as naturally as she could at Justin Wilmore.

'It's a wonderful costume!' She tried to make her tone light and without special significance. 'I feel just like the character – like Fiora – in the opera.'

'You look just like her too.' Her host passed a hand over his face as though brushing away some mist from before his eyes. 'You even have the perfect mixture of innocence and guilt in your expression. How did you do that? Were you just thinking yourself into the role of Fiora?'

'Not really.' She was aware that Elliot Cheam had now followed her down the stairs and was standing just behind her. 'Mr. Cheam seemed to think I was taking a liberty in wearing the costume, which made me feel momentarily guilty, I suppose. But, as I recalled that the suggestion that I should try it on had come entirely from you, I decided I had every right to feel innocent.' And, glancing over her shoulder, she gave Elliot Cheam a defiant little smile.

'Clever, clever girl,' he said. And she knew he was not referring to the way in which she had impersonated a stage character. 'Come and meet our neighbour, Sara Fernie. She will appreciate the – theatricality of the moment.'

Feeling somehow that she was still in a slightly false position, Joanna did her best to look at ease and, accompanied by the two men, she went into the drawing-

33

room where a tall, dark girl in a stunning white and emerald green dress was standing looking out of the window.

She turned as they came in and said, 'Ell—' then she stopped and cried, 'Oh, what a gorgeous costume! Wherever did it come from?'

'From Uncle Justin's collection,' stated Elliot, giving the impression that he was biting off the ends of his words rather sharply. 'Miss Ransome came to see the collection, and somehow ended up wearing some of it. Miss Ransome, this is Sara Fernie. I expect you've heard of her.'

'Of course.' Joanna rather diffidently extended a hand towards the well-known actress who had appeared so successfully in more than one of Elliot Cheam's productions.

But, either not noticing the hand or deliberately ignoring it, Sara Fernie walked round Joanna inspecting her from all angles.

'It's gorgeous,' she repeated, as though only the dress mattered and the girl who was wearing it hardly existed. 'I wonder if it would fit me.'

'I'm afraid you're not likely to find out.' Justin Wilmore's tone was perfectly pleasant and courteous, but there was no mistaking the decision in his voice.

'Why not?' Sara Fernie smiled at him, a little challengingly.

'Because that is a Trangoni costume. And I don't let people try on the Trangoni costumes in the usual way.'

'But you let *her*.'

'With Miss Ransome it is a little different. She is going to sing the role for which this dress was created.'

'Oh—' the other girl seemed to take in Joanna as a person for the first time – 'you're a singer, then? A professional singer, I take it?'

'No. I'm a last-year student at St. Cecilia's College, and we're putting on a production of—'

'Uncle Justin, I call that mean!' Sara Fernie suddenly laughed and turned on her host the full and impressive battery of her charm. 'You allow a student to run around in this dress and you won't even let me try it on!'

'She is not running around in it,' replied Justin Wilmore. 'She put it on to please me and—'

'And now I'm going upstairs to take it off,' stated Joanna. 'I can't tell you how much I've enjoyed hearing you talk of the part I'm to play, Mr. Wilmore. And actually wearing Trangoni's own costume for a few minutes has been a sort of inspiration. But now I really must go. My aunt will be expecting me and—'

Somehow she found it impossible to discover the right sentence on which to make a graceful exit. But she had been backing towards the door while she spoke and, on the reference to her aunt, she managed to gather together enough dignity and resolution to make her escape.

As she went she heard Sara say amusedly, 'Funny, gauche little thing. Does she really expect to play a part on a stage?'

'That's her story,' Elliot Cheam's voice replied lightly. And then Joanna fled up the stairs.

She found her way to the bedroom again, and was relieved to find the invaluable Mrs. Trimble, apparently still in attendance.

'Oh, Mrs. Trimble!' There was such a thankful sound to that exclamation that she realized she must add something else. So she hastily asked, 'Who is Sara Fernie? I mean – of course I know she's a well-known actress. But is she also a relation of Mr. Wilmore's?'

'No, miss, she certainly is not. What made you think that?'

'She addressed him as "Uncle Justin".'

'Oh—' the housekeeper smiled rather grimly. 'Well, I daresay she would like to be his niece. By marriage, of course.'

'You mean she's hoping to marry Mr. Cheam?'

'That is my view, Miss Ransome. Though of course my guess isn't any better than anyone else's,' said Mrs. Trimble, her expression, however, making it clear that she thought it was.

'I should think,' observed Joanna, as she carefully divested herself of the beautiful costume, 'that they would just about suit each other.'

'Would you?' Mrs. Trimble looked surprised. 'She's pretty hard, under all that charm.'

'That's what I meant,' Joanna said a little dryly. 'Isn't he pretty hard too?'

'No.' The housekeeper took the costume from her and laid it on the bed, while Joanna slipped into her own clothes again. 'He's impulsive and hot-tempered, which is quite a different thing. Many's the time he got into trouble over that when he was a schoolboy. But there was never anything mean or deliberately unkind about him. And he didn't mind saying when he was sorry. You can forgive a lot for that.'

'Ye-es,' agreed Joanna, who was trying to visualize Elliot Cheam as a schoolboy, and failing. 'Did he often come here, Mrs. Trimble?'

'He lived here. It was his home. His parents were out East, and he came here for all his holidays. Mr. Wil-

36

more was closer to him than his own father. And Mr. Elliot, who is so quick and impulsive, always had the idea that his uncle's quiet, easy-going manner laid him open to being imposed upon. Even as a little boy he used to have some sort of idea of protecting him. But there, I'm talking too much!'

'It's all tremendously interesting,' Joanna assured her. 'And it's been a wonderful visit.'

'Mr. Wilmore is expecting you to stay to tea, Miss Ransome.'

'Is he?' She was divided between the delightful prospect of further conversation with Mr. Wilmore and the nervous conviction that she would show to poor advantage in the company of Elliot Cheam and his leading lady. 'You don't think they – I mean he – might feel I was overstaying my welcome?'

'No, miss, I don't. Mr. Wilmore took a fancy to you – I could see that – and I'm sure he wouldn't want you to go away without so much as a cup of tea.'

So Joanna stifled her misgivings and went down to the drawing-room once more, where her host made her very welcome over tea; and Elliot and Sara – if they paid little attention to her – at least said nothing further to make her feel uncomfortable.

'If there is anything more you feel you need to know about the role of Fiora, don't hesitate to come and ask me,' Mr. Wilmore said. 'I'm afraid what you got this afternoon was little more than a jumble of general impressions.'

'Mr. Wilmore, it was probably the best informal lesson on the role that I'm ever likely to have,' Joanna assured him gratefully. 'I wasn't proposing to impose on your time again. But if I do have a query—'

'Then you must let me know. There would be no

question of imposing on me. If you visit your aunt often, please come and see me some time.'

'I – I should love to,' stammered Joanna.

'Sometimes people from the musical world come down here for a week-end or a few days. More to examine the collection than to see me, I daresay—' he smiled whimsically, 'it might be of help for you to meet one or two of them. A young artist can't have too many friendly contacts among established musicians. Now, how are you going to get back to your aunt's place?'

'I'll walk,' said Joanna.

'I'll drive her,' stated Elliot Cheam at the same moment.

'There's really no need!'

'You mean you don't want to trust yourself to my driving?' He grinned at her suddenly, and she had to make an effort to remember just how much she disliked him. 'I'll take great care of you.'

'Yes, please do,' said his uncle. 'We are already good friends, I hope.'

So Joanna repeated her thanks to her host, said her good-byes and went out with Elliot Cheam to the car which had so inauspiciously started their acquaintance.

It was quite a short drive, of course, giving little time for well-considered conversation. But Joanna felt she must seize this opportunity to set herself right in his eyes, if only partially.

'Mr. Cheam—' her voice sounded more nervous than she had intended – 'I do understand your wanting to protect your very kind uncle from people who might impose on him. But, truly, that isn't my intention. He's so fine and – and courteous and *good* that I wouldn't dream of it. It just so happens that my aunt is a neighbour of his, and she had a chance to ask him if I could come and see his collection because of this modest assignment of mine. He agreed and – and I came, and I was as stunned as anyone else when the rest followed. It's all because I have – I mean, he thinks I have – some odd likeness to the artist he admired so much in his youth. But so far as I'm concerned—'

'Take a deep breath and count ten,' he advised her. And, glancing at him, she saw he was smiling as he looked straight ahead down the road.

'You mean I'm making so many excuses it all sounds phoney?'

'No, I mean you were running out of breath. And anyway, you've justified yourself sufficiently to make me feel a bit of a heel. It *could* all have happened just as you said, and I'll take your word for it at the moment. I'll even apologize, if you like. But for my part, let me say I'm devoted to the old boy, who is both kindly and unworldly, and I make it my business to see that no one – and I mean no one – gets the better of his good heart and romantic disposition. No hard feelings, I hope?'

'No hard feelings,' agreed Joanna, swallowing down part, if not quite all, of her resentment. He could, she felt, have made somewhat more handsome amends – particularly after what Mrs. Trimble had said about his not minding saying if he were sorry – but they had arrived outside Aunt Georgina's bungalow by now. So she bade him good-bye and got out of the car.

She was sorry to see Aunt Georgina's front room curtain flutter unmistakably as she walked up the path, and she hoped Elliot Cheam had driven off before he could also note this and probably cast Aunt Georgina as a fellow-conspirator.

Her aunt did not even try to conceal her interest in every detail of the visit. And, longing as she was to go over it all again herself, Joanna gave a spirited account of her afternoon.

'He let you *wear* one of the Trangoni costumes?' Even Aunt Georgina was impressed. 'That can't have happened to many people.'

'To no one else, if I understood the housekeeper and the nephew aright,' Joanna said.

'Why did you put the housekeeper before the nephew?' asked Aunt Georgina, who missed very little.

'I – don't know.' Joanna looked surprised. 'Except that I liked the housekeeper, I suppose,'

'But not the nephew—'

'Not really. But then I don't think he liked me. He was unnecessarily suspicious about my motives in coming to see his uncle.'

'It would be unwise to quarrel with any member of the family,' observed her aunt.

'I didn't *quarrel* with him. At least—' Joanna recalled one or two things she and Elliot Cheam had said to each other and was suddenly unwilling to develop that theme. Instead, she said hastily, 'Mr. Wilmore told me to come and see him again if there were any points on which I wanted to know more.'

'Then you must find some points,' stated Miss Ransome without scruple.

'Oh, Aunt Georgina! I wouldn't want anyone to think I was imposing on—'

'No one would be so silly,' replied her aunt, who had not met Elliot Cheam. 'Now come and have your supper.'

So Joanna had her supper. An absolutely splendid

one, since Aunt Georgina had suffered from enough school meals in her day to pamper herself somewhat now that she did her own housekeeping. And after a gloriously peaceful night, Joanna woke to the sound of distant farm noises and the full recollection of all that had happened yesterday.

For some minutes she lay watching the sunlight on the green and white wallpaper of Aunt Georgina's guest-room, recalling afresh the extraordinary experience of being linked personally with the famous Emilia Trangoni. And if, for a moment or two, her thoughts lingered not so blissfully on Elliot Cheam, presently she had incorporated even him into the glorious whole.

Back home again, Joanna once more had to give a full account of her visit. Though her mother's interjections were more to the effect that it was quite natural for Mr. Wilmore to want to see her in the dress, and that the nephew sounded very disagreeable indeed, and quite unworthy of being remembered.

From long experience, Joanna knew better than to attempt to modify her mother's strictures. So she left the subject and during the ensuing week devoted herself to the role of Fiora, trying to incorporate in her idea of the part all that she had learned during her visit to the Justin Wilmore collection.

As a result, when she was first called on to rehearse the first act with the rest of the cast, she earned an astonishing degree of approval from both producer and conductor.

'Joanna, you must have done a lot of work on this!' The producer, not usually lavish with his praise, patted her shoulder approvingly. 'You have a real idea of the part. And yet you couldn't ever have heard a performance of it. Unless in Italy – or somewhere

41

else abroad?'

'No, I never heard a performance,' Joanna agreed. 'But I love the role and have a – a sort of *feeling* for it.'

'Well, keep up the feeling, and you'll do well.' The producer laughed. 'Pity the voice isn't bigger,' he added to her singing teacher, who happened to be standing by. 'But she's young and it will develop.'

'Of course.' Joanna's singing teacher, who disliked all producers on principle, spoke coldly. And later she added to Joanna, 'That's the worst of these modern producers. No idea about real singing, as such, and always trying to push young singers beyond their natural bent.'

'Do you think this role is pushing me beyond my natural bent?' inquired Joanna anxiously.

'Not if you deploy your vocal resources carefully. Anyway, don't take any notice of me today. I think I've got 'flu coming on, and it makes everything seem vile.'

Joanna expressed suitable sympathy. But her teacher certainly did look ill, and she was not surprised when, on arriving for her lesson on Monday morning, she found that the poor lady was away on sick leave.

As it happened, the first cast for 'The Love of Three Kings' was being rehearsed that day, so Joanna found herself unexpectedly free. It was true, of course, that she could put in plenty of general study on her own account, but the prospect of a completely free day was suddenly too tempting to resist. She decided to go to the West End and do some shopping, and then later in the day she would work specially hard at home.

It was a cool but sunny morning, and she enjoyed some shop-gazing and made a few purchases. Then, after a modest lunch, she was just thinking of going home when, as she sauntered down Shaftesbury Avenue, she was brought up short by the sight of a familiar face. There, outside the Coronet Theatre, was an arresting photograph of Sara Fernie.

Beside it, printed in large letters, was the information that on the following Wednesday at eight-thirty there would be the first performance of a new play by Thurston Goodman – Producer, Elliot Cheam.

A good deal intrigued, and feeling almost personally involved, Joanna lingered to absorb every detail. She would certainly manage to come one evening – though not, of course, to the first night. Perhaps she and her mother might—

'Hello,' said a familiar voice behind her. 'What are you doing star-gazing? Shouldn't you be busy studying "The Love of Three Kings"?'

'Why—' she turned to greet Elliot Cheam with more pleasure than she would have believed possible. 'I just happen to have the day free, because my teacher is ill and—'

'Do you want to come in to the dress rehearsal?' he asked unexpectedly.

'*Could* I? Do you mean it's this afternoon?'

'It's been going on all day,' he replied wearily. 'We've just had a short break for lunch. Perhaps you'd like to come and see just how hard the real professional has to work.'

'If that's a nasty crack at my student status—' she began, half laughing.

'No, no. Don't be so ready to jump down my throat. Everyone is being temperamental today – including me, I shouldn't wonder – and I could do with someone

43

around who isn't involved. Come along.'

He put a careless arm round her shoulders and ushered her into the theatre. While Joanna – not quite sure what had hit her – tried to conceal the immense gratification she felt at this totally unexpected invitation.

He conducted her into the half-lit auditorium, which looked strangely dreary without audience or full lighting. There were several people scattered about, one or two of whom called out a greeting or question to Elliot Cheam.

'Coming, coming,' he said, in answer to the most insistent of these. And then, to Joanna, 'Stay as long as you like, but if you get tired of it before the end, you can slip out by that side door there. Enjoy yourself. Which is more than I shall do,' he added gloomily as he left her.

But nothing would have induced Joanna to leave the place once the rehearsal had started. It was more or less a complete run-through, with few interruptions but a great deal of often acrimonious discussion between the acts.

Sara Fernie, she reluctantly realized, was nothing short of brilliant and, so long as she could have her own way, she fulfilled every demand the part made upon her. But once or twice she was at odds with both author and producer, and Joanna became more and more astonished to find how much venom could be put into the one word, 'Darling—'

She sensed that Elliot Cheam was controlling his temper with some difficulty, particularly when Sara actually turned her back on him while he was speaking to her. As for the wretched author, if he did not literally tear out his hair in handfuls, he gave the impression of being ready to do so at any moment.

In spite of all this, Joanna – who had an extremely keen stage sense – was enchanted with the play, and was so excited at the end that she actually followed one or two people on to the stage, and unexpectedly found herself beside the unhappy author.

'It's a marvellous play!' she exclaimed. 'It simply can't fail.'

'What do *you* know about it?' asked the nerve-torn author fretfully. 'Who are you, anyway?'

'I'm part of the general public. And we're all going to love it,' Joanna informed him confidently.

Whereupon Elliot Cheam laughed and said, 'Well, I'm glad someone is pleased with our efforts, and in a good temper about it all.' Then he actually slipped his arm round her again and added, 'You'd better come out to dinner with me. I could do with some of that irrepressible optimism.'

'But—' suddenly Joanna *knew* that Sara was staring at her in a hostile manner, even though she had her back to the leading lady – 'weren't you going with Sara?' she whispered.

'Yes. But she's turned me down,' he whispered back again, as though they were a couple of conspirators. 'Please come – and bolster up my sagging morale.'

He was half laughing, of course. She was sure of that. But she was equally sure that there was a serious undercurrent somewhere in all this.

'I would have to phone my mother. She's expecting me back—'

'Come to my office. You can phone from there,' he said.

So she went with him to his office, where he shoved the telephone across the desk to her and then slumped into a chair opposite and began to make rapid notes on a pad.

'Mother—' Joanna cleared her throat a little self-consciously. 'It's me – Joanna. I shan't be in until late-ish this evening. I'm going out to dinner – with Elliot Cheam,' she added, unaware that she dropped her voice slightly.

'With whom, dear?' inquired her mother's voice interestedly.

'Elliot Cheam,' repeated Joanna unwillingly.

'Elliot Cheam? That horrible nephew of old Mr. Wilmore, do you mean?'

'Oh, Mother, he's *not* horrible—' She stopped then, and it was Elliot who cleared his throat this time.

'Don't mind me,' he said, without looking up. And Joanna giggled suddenly and irrepressibly, partly from nervousness and partly because she thought the situation really funny.

Apparently he did too. For when she finally replaced the receiver he grinned across at her and asked, 'Where did Mother get that idea, you naughty girl?'

'I can't imagine,' she replied demurely.

'Well, wait here. I've got a few last-minute instructions to give,' he informed her as he got up and went towards the door. But, to her astonishment, he touched her shoulder lightly as he passed her and said, 'Thanks for coming with me this evening.'

Alone in the office, Joanna sat very still and tried to readjust herself to a new state of affairs. The Elliot Cheam of this afternoon and evening seemed a very different person from the one who had been so resentful of her presence in his uncle's house. Indeed, she was surprised to remember now, she had sprung un-hesitatingly to his defence when her mother had criticized him.

'One shouldn't judge too hastily,' she told herself. And then she wondered if she were judging too hastily in assuming that Elliot's friendliness could be taken at its face value. It was possible, of course, that he had invited her out to dinner more to annoy Sara than to please herself. But before she could examine this unwelcome possibility further he came back.

'Ready?' He shut and locked one or two drawers, pushed some papers into a leather case which he tucked under his arm, and then ushered her out of the room and presently into the street, where the famous green car was waiting.

'Have you any preferences about restaurants?' he inquired, as he took his place in the driving seat beside her.

'No. I just like good food,' she assured him without inhibition. 'And I love being taken out. It doesn't happen all that often.'

'Doesn't it?' He smiled at her curiously. 'I should have thought a pretty girl like you would be a good deal in demand.'

'Oh, I go out with fellow-students, of course. Coffee bars and that sort of thing, you know. But that isn't quite the same thing as being taken out to dinner by a famous producer, is it?'

'I suppose it isn't.' He looked amused. 'Well, we'll see if we can improve on the coffee bar.'

They did. He took her to a deceptively quiet-looking restaurant where the food was superb and the wines much more choice than Joanna's unsophisticated palate ever discovered. It was obvious that he was a frequent and valued customer. And, once their meal had been chosen, he sat back with an air of relaxation

47

and regarded her with something like satisfaction.

'Tell me about yourself,' he said unexpectedly. 'You harp a good deal on the fact that you're only a student. Have you had any sort of professional experience at all?'

'If you count solo engagements with one or two quite well-known choirs – yes. And I've been in several of our end-of-term productions, which earned me nice notices from some of the critics. And then I had a short season with the Planton Touring Company at the beginning of the year—'

'Did you?' he looked interested. 'Chorus or small parts?'

'Secondary roles, but I understudied two leading roles.'

'But no one conveniently sprained an ankle and gave you a chance to jump in?'

'I'm afraid not.' She laughed contritely. 'Not that one wishes ill to a colleague, of course, but—'

'Some people do,' he assured her.

'I don't think so,' she said seriously. 'Not if they are reasonably well-wishing, I mean.'

'And how many people are reasonably well-wishing, do you suppose, in a competitive profession like this?'

'Quite a number of them. Just as in any other profession,' Joanna replied with spirit.

'Don't you believe it!' His sceptical laugh was an unwelcome reminder of the way he had doubted her good faith towards his uncle.

'You distrust people too easily,' she told him coolly. 'And anyway, you're feeling jaundiced just now because some people were horrible at the dress rehearsal.'

'Good of you to explain me to myself.' He looked amused again. Then he glanced across the restaurant and observed, 'Why, there are the Warrenders!'

'You mean *Oscar* Warrender?' Joanna gazed in open wonder at the tall, commanding-looking man who had just come in and was accepting, as of right, the near-homage of the head waiter who rushed forward to receive him and his companion. 'And the girl must be Anthea Benton!' Joanna drew in her breath on an admiring little gasp. 'Fancy looking like that as well as being able to sing as she does!'

'Yes, she's rarely gifted,' Elliot Cheam agreed. And then as the lovely girl in the white mink jacket glanced across, smiled suddenly and waved, Joanna's companion rose to his feet.

Instinctively she did the same as the Warrenders came across, for she felt, as she swallowed an excited lump in her throat, that here indeed was a glimpse of operatic Olympus.

'Why, Elliot, how nice to see you! How is the new show coming along?' Anthea Warrender touched Elliot's hand in a friendly way and then smiled at the dazzled Joanna as Elliot made the introductions.

'You'd better ask Joanna. She was at the dress rehearsal,' Elliot said, to Joanna's astonishment. 'I've been too near it for too long to be any judge myself. Now I'm just in a sort of unhappy, knuckle-chewing limbo until the first night is over.'

'One knows the feeling,' said the famous conductor, speaking for the first time, though he didn't look as though he had ever chewed a knuckle in his life. 'What is your opinion, Miss Joanna?'

Miss Joanna, who had never in her wildest moments imagined being addressed in these terms by Oscar Warrender, somehow cleared her thoughts enough to say, 'As a mere member of the public, I thought it brilliant. Both the play itself and the way it's produced and acted.'

'Members of the public are never "mere",' declared Anthea Warrender with a laugh. 'Particularly on first nights. We're all terrified of you then, because it's your verdict that counts.'

'Joanna knows the feeling to a certain extent too,' Elliot said. 'She also is a singer.'

'Oh, please!' Joanna flushed to the roots of her hair. 'Not even to be mentioned in this company. I'm nothing but a student.'

'My dear, we're all students to begin with,' Anthea assured her kindly. 'And a very happy time of one's career it can be, too. I loved my student days – except when Oscar was being mean to me!'

'I was never mean to you,' said her husband imperturbably. 'Only healthily strict. Which is why you are such a great artist today. So you're a singing student, Miss Joanna?' Joanna was both pleased and frightened to have his attention on her again. 'What do you sing?'

'I'm a lyric soprano,' said Joanna timidly.

'Yes?' The great man's tone was not discouraging.

'I – I hope to sing in opera one day. But I haven't got further than a little touring experience and our end-of-term productions at St. Cecilia's.'

'Let me see – they're doing "L'Amore dei Tre Re" this term, aren't they?'

'Yes.' Joanna nodded, somewhat awed that the small doings of her college should actually find a place in Oscar Warrender's famous memory.

'And what part are you taking?'

'Fi-Fiora. In the second cast, though,' she amplified

hastily, which seemed to amuse him for some reason.

'Well, you will be following in some distinguished footsteps,' he said, not unkindly. 'And that reminds me—' he turned once more to Elliot – 'we're going down to visit your uncle, the week-end after next. Shall you be there?'

'I don't think so.' Elliot sounded regretful. 'I doubt if I could get away so early in the run. Unless, of course, it's a flop and closes within a week.'

'None of us would want that, even for the pleasure of your company at the Manor,' Anthea declared with a mock shudder.

'Anyway, it's not going to be a flop,' Joanna asserted positively. 'It's going to be a great success.'

'There you are, Elliot. The public has spoken,' said Warrender amusedly. 'Good luck.' And he and Anthea went over to their table, while Joanna propped her chin on her hands, gazed happily at Elliot Cheam and said,

'I'd no idea he was like that!'

'Like what?'

'Well, approachable and kind. I always heard he was so difficult and an absolute tyrant.'

'He's mellowed a bit with the years, I suppose,' Elliot said consideringly. 'That's her doing. She's one of the nicest women on God's earth, and Warrender adores her in his way. But that doesn't prevent his being a tyrant still in the opera house, to her or anyone else.'

'Do they know your uncle very well?' Joanna asked with interest.

'Yes. Why?' Suddenly his tone was guarded, she noticed, and the realization chilled and embarrassed her.

'I'm not planning to go down there during their visit, if that's what you're thinking,' she told him sharply. 'Why do you have to be unpleasant and suspicious every time I presume to mention your uncle?'

'I wasn't being unpleasant and suspicious.' He sounded slightly on the defensive. 'The idea just crossed my mind that—'

'Well, it can cross back again,' she told him tartly. 'Whatever you may want to think, I'm not the sort of girl—'

'I know, I know. I'm sorry. Take no notice of me. I'm in an impossible mood, and I shouldn't really have inflicted myself on you or anyone else tonight.'

'Yes, you should.' She was instantly contrite. 'I ought to have remembered that you've had a beast of a day. And I'm terribly glad you took me out tonight. I wouldn't have missed this for anything.'

'Really?' And when she nodded, he said, 'You're a nice child.' And then suddenly he smothered an irrepresible yawn.

'You're dead tired,' she exclaimed. 'And no wonder. We'd better go now.'

'Don't you want coffee first?'

'No, thank you. And nor do you. You'll sleep better without it, and sleep is what you want.'

He looked for a moment as though he might make some amused protest. But then weariness seemed to wash over him like a wave, and he murmured, 'If you're sure you don't mind.'

'I don't mind anything, so long as you won't think I would try to muscle in on the Warrenders' week-end at your uncle's place.'

'Forget it,' he said impatiently. Then he called for

the bill and, having paid it, followed her out of the restaurant into the street.

'Drive carefully,' she said, lightly touching his arm, 'and thank you for a lovely, lovely evening.'

'I'm taking you home first.'

'Indeed you're not.' She smiled up at him. 'You ought to be in bed now. And I'm getting this bus that's just coming along. It passes the end of my road.'

'You're sure?'

'Of course I'm sure.' She swung herself on to the platform of the bus, then waved and called back over her shoulder, 'Thank you again, and good luck for Wednesday!'

She saw, as the bus swung round a corner, that he was still looking after her, with a smile that somehow warmed her heart.

'I can't believe it all!' she told herself as she made her way to the front seat in the bus. 'I just can't believe it. Oh, I do hope Mother's still up. I just *have* to tell someone all about it!'

Fortunately, her mother was indeed up. In fact, she came running into the hall as Joanna opened the front door, and it was she who first began to pour out an excited tale.

'Joanna, the most wonderful thing! You'll never believe it. Mr. Wilmore telephoned about an hour ago. What a *nice* man. A gentleman, as Georgina said. He wanted to speak to you—'

'To me? What about?'

'Well, I'm just telling you, dear, if you'll let me finish. I explained that you were out, of course, and he asked me to give you a message. He wants you to go down there the week-end after next—'

'Oh, no!' There was more dismay than pleasure

in Joanna's tone.

'Wait a minute, that isn't all. He says the *Warrenders* will be there and he would like you to meet them—'

'I've met them,' said Joanna dazedly.

'Don't be silly, dear! Of course you haven't. I'm speaking of Sir Oscar Warrender and his wife—'

'So am I,' murmured Joanna, but her mother went on. 'He said if it was not convenient for your aunt to have you he would be delighted for you to stay at the Manor. So I said immediately that I knew your aunt would be away—'

'But she won't.' Joanna looked bewildered.

'No, of course she won't. But I said she would. You don't suppose I was going to let you miss a chance like that, do you? You'll be staying at Wilmore Manor at the same time as the Warrenders – think of that! No one would *believe* that things could fall out just that way, would they?'

CHAPTER THREE

JOANNA gazed at her mother in open dismay. As Mrs Ransome had just said, no one would believe – least of all Elliot Cheam – that 'things could fall out just that way.'

'I can't go, Mother,' she said rather distractedly.

'*Can't go?*' Her mother looked both astonished and annoyed. 'Of course you can go. It's the chance of a lifetime. What were you going to do the week-end after next that cannot be put off, for goodness' sake?'

'Nothing. At least, nothing I can remember.' Joanna pushed back her hair from her forehead with both hands. 'It isn't that. It's – oh, let me explain—'

'Well, come in and sit down first. I was so excited I just had to rush out to tell you at once. And now you're behaving as though I'd given you bad news. I don't understand you, Joanna. You never used to be temperamental and difficult. Being given this important role hasn't gone to your head, I hope.'

'No – no, of course not.' Joanna followed her mother into the dining-room, where she was oddly touched to see a vacuum jug of hot chocolate and a cup and saucer standing at the end of the table.

'I thought you might like a hot drink.' Her mother indicated the jug a little timidly, as though her daughter had suddenly become so unpredictable that she might resent, rather than welcome, the attention.

'Oh, Mother, how sweet of you!' Joanna smiled gratefully. At which her mother's face cleared and she looked like a child who was beginning to think that

55

everything might be all right, after all.

'Now tell me.' Mrs. Ransome sat back in her chair, an eager expression on her face. 'First of all, was it a good evening?'

'Lovely, thank you.'

'Even though you had to go with that horrid young man?'

'He's not a horrid young man. And anyway, he had already given me one delightful treat.' She explained about being unexpectedly invited in to the dress rehearsal, and how this had presently led to her being asked out to dinner.

'Well, I suppose you couldn't refuse when he'd already been nice to you,' her mother conceded.

'I didn't want to refuse.' Joanna was a little surprised to remember how eager she had been, on the contrary, to accept. 'We were getting on splendidly by then. He took me to a perfectly charming restaurant, and we were just enjoying our meal when – I know it sounds improbable – in came the Warrenders.'

'Then you *have* met them? I thought you were making some kind of joke.'

'No, I meant it literally. They came over to our table and Elliot – Mr. Cheam – introduced me and they were both very pleasant to me.'

'Darling, what a delightful coincidence!' Mrs. Ransome was enchanted. 'That you actually *know* them already! They'll be so pleased to find you too are staying at the Manor. I thought you meant—'

'Just a moment, it's not so simple as that,' Joanna insisted. 'They said – that is Sir Oscar said – that they were going down to stay with Elliot's uncle the weekend after next, and asked if he too would be there. Elliot explained he would be too much tied up with his new production and—'

'What a pity you didn't already know you'd been invited. If you'd been able to announce that in fact *you* would be there it would have caused quite a sensation,' declared Mrs. Ransome.

'Yes, it would have caused no end of a sensation,' Joanna agreed rather grimly. 'Elliot would have been furious.'

'Why? Just because he couldn't go too? What a dog in the manger! He's just as unpleasant as I thought, after all.'

'No, he isn't. He's *nice*,' Joanna stated firmly. 'But as I told you before, he has the idea that people try to impose on his uncle – to cadge things from him – because he's so naturally kind and easy-going. Oh, he's a bit exaggerated about it, I suppose. In fact, of course he is. But it all stems from a genuine wish to protect someone he's very fond of.'

'I call that silly,' her mother replied impatiently. 'Why not leave his uncle to look after himself? He's a grown man, isn't he? Not like a woman left all on her own.' And Mrs. Ransome glanced instinctively at her own pretty reflection in the mirror opposite her.

Joanna abandoned any further academic discussion on this point and went on determinedly with her story.

'When the Warrenders had gone to their table we naturally spoke a few words about them, and I asked if they knew his uncle well. He immediately looked withdrawn and suspicious—'

'I said he was unpleasant!' interjected her mother triumphantly.

'—and asked why I wanted to know. If he hadn't been tired and irritable after a gruelling rehearsal I

57

doubt if he would have reacted quite that way—'

'Yes, he would. That's the way that kind of man *does* react.'

'—but anyway, I snapped back in my turn, I'm afraid—'

'And quite right too!'

'—and said he needn't think I was trying to muscle in on the Warrenders' week-end at Wilmore Manor, because such an idea had never entered my head, and I didn't behave that way anyway. He apologized then.'

'And so he should!' declared her mother. 'And what a slap in the face for him when you do turn up.'

'But I can't turn up! Don't you see,' said Joanna patiently, 'that's the point? The very fact that I took up such an indignant stand about being unjustly suspected makes this occasion, of all occasions, the one when I just can't go.'

'But he won't be there.' Her mother looked obstinate.

'How do you know he won't be there?'

'You've just said he won't.' With unerring accuracy, Mrs. Ransome dredged up from her daughter's story what she considered to be the one salient point. 'You said he told Sir Oscar he wouldn't be there because he would be busy with this silly play of his.'

Joanna thought of saying that it was not a silly play – that, in fact, it was quite a brilliant play – but she knew that, in her present mood, her mother was determined to find nothing good in Elliot Cheam and all his works.

Instead she said slowly, 'It's true he did say he almost certainly couldn't be there. But then he'd be bound to hear about it eventually.'

'Why? Does that poor old uncle of his have to give

him an account of everyone who visits the place?'

'No, of course not! These things come out in ordinary conversation. And I couldn't bear to have him discover that, after I'd taken up such a virtuous stand about being unjustly suspected, off I went and turned up there after all.'

'Darling, you are adopting the most ridiculous attitude about it all,' exclaimed her mother impatiently. 'Who *is* this Elliot Cheam, anyway? Why should you bother about his views or let him dictate your actions? The invitation came from Mr. Wilmore to you – for a week-end that might give you the most valuable contacts in your career. And you're prepared to throw away this priceless opportunity because you're frightened of some disagreeable young man.'

'I'm *not* frightened of him.'

'Well, you're behaving exactly as though you were. And what about Mr. Wilmore, come to that? How will *he* feel if you just throw back his invitation in his face?'

'I wasn't going to do any such thing,' muttered Joanna protestingly. But she did look rather shaken. For after all, it was, as her mother said, the chance of a lifetime – and so very kindly meant. 'If I could somehow let Elliot Cheam know—' She was still speaking under her breath, but her mother caught her last words.

'Why?' she demanded scornfully. 'Do you have to ask his permission before you dare to approach his uncle?'

'No. It's just—' and then Joanna realized that they were back on the same circular track again, and that unless she put an end to the conversation they would continue with argument and counter-argument indefinitely.

'I can't make a decision at the moment,' she declared, drinking the rest of her chocolate and setting down the cup with an air of determination. 'I'm too excited and – and tired – and bewildered with so much happening all at once. I'll have to think things over. If there's any way of accepting this wonderful invitation, I'll do so, of course. But I shall stay with Aunt Georgina. I couldn't possibly stay at the Manor.'

'It would be perfectly respectable,' said her mother naïvely. 'With an elderly housekeeper and other guests and all that.'

'Oh, Mother, you're a darling!' Joanna kissed her and laughed. 'I was not worrying about my reputation.'

'No. You were just worrying about what that tiresome young man might think,' retorted her mother. 'I don't know why he has suddenly become so important to you. Don't get any silly ideas about him, will you? He doesn't sound at all the kind of person I should like you to get fond of.'

'There isn't the slightest danger of that!' Joanna assured her. 'And anyway, I think he's a good deal involved with Sara Fernie, his leading lady. She's very good in this new play, by the way. You and I must go and see it some time next week. You would enjoy it.'

'Well—' Mrs. Ransome, who adored the theatre, obviously found the prospect attractive, even if it would mean coming under the same roof as the despised Elliot Cheam. 'Let's see first what the reviews are like.'

And on that she and her daughter bade each other good night and went to their rooms – Joanna at least to sit on the side of her bed in deep thought, divided between the overwhelming temptation to accept Mr.

Wilmore's invitation at any cost, and the almost pathological fear of increasing Elliot Cheam's unfair suspicions.

'There *must* be a perfectly sensible and civilized way of dealing with it,' she told herself. 'I suppose I could phone him—' But the idea of troubling him with her small concerns when he was so much involved in his own work would be ridiculous. And even more ridiculous would be the implication that she thought him entitled to be consulted at all. There would be no way of putting it which would not sound as though she thought she needed his permission to go down to Wilmore Manor. And that would be the height of absurdity.

Although she had argued each point in the recent discussion, she had not been unaffected by her mother's viewpoint. And, reflecting quietly now on her own, she did think that perhaps she had been showing an exaggerated regard for what Elliot Cheam thought or said. After all, he was nothing to her. At least – almost nothing. Except insofar as one preferred to have the good opinion of anyone one liked and respected – even moderately.

'I'll work out a plan of action tomorrow,' she decided. '*Of course* I couldn't miss a chance like this. And anyway, as Mother said, what about Mr. Wilmore's feelings? He might be really hurt if I refused his kind gesture.'

That thought seemed to weight the scales much more heavily on the side of her doing what she was longing to do. And, on that cheering thought, Joanna went to bed and to sleep.

Both she and her mother overslept the next morning, and Joanna had no time to do anything but snatch a

61

hasty breakfast and rush off to the College. Here she found that her singing teacher was not only still away but, according to report, likely to be so for some while. Consequently there had to be some change in her scheme of studies. Her singing lessons were, of necessity, transferred to another teacher – excellent in his way, but not at all temperamentally in tune with Joanna.

This made her nervous and strained, for the relationship between singing student and teacher is always a very personal and delicately balanced one. And, when she came to a rehearsal of the opera during the afternoon, she was not at all at her best.

'Nothing like so good as the other day,' the producer told her with a frown. 'What's the matter? Have you been slacking?'

'A – a little, perhaps,' said Joanna, thinking guiltily of the free day she had enjoyed yesterday.

'Well, don't,' he advised her grimly. 'It shows.'

She went home rather chastened, to find her mother still making such happy plans about the proposed week-end that she realized she must take a stand one way or the other. And why should she not go, anyway? She was certainly not feeling in a mood to pass over any chance of learning more about her part and once more confounding the producer with her inner knowledge!

'I shall phone Aunt Georgina right away,' she declared.

'Why? I've already arranged for you to stay at Wilmore Manor,' replied her mother plaintively. 'You'll make me look silly if you show that Georgina will be there to put you up, after what I said.'

'Nothing like so silly as we should both look if we let

your story stand and then Mr. Wilmore happened to run into her over that week-end,' retorted Joanna. And she went to the telephone and dialled her aunt's number.

Mrs. Ransome watched with some anxiety while Joanna talked to Aunt Georgina. Then gradually, as the drift of the conversation began to come clear to her, she smiled and looked rather as a very nice kitten might have looked when a bowl of cream turned over unexpectedly in front of it.

'You won't believe it—' Joanna slowly hung up the receiver – 'but Aunt Georgina *is* going to be away that week-end.'

'I'm not a bit surprised,' replied Mrs. Ransome, who had her own very personal brand of superstition. (For instance, she always read What the Stars Foretold, but only believed the bits that promised what she wanted.) 'It is Meant to Be,' she added contentedly.

'It's nothing of the kind,' replied Joanna rather crossly. But then, as though something stronger than herself impelled her, she picked up the receiver again and dialled the number which Mr. Wilmore had left with her mother.

Mrs. Trimble's voice answered. But she fetched Mr. Wilmore immediately when she realized who was speaking. And in a few moments Joanna found herself explaining how truly happy she was to accept his invitation and that, since her aunt would be away, if he *really* meant he would like her to stay at Wilmore Manor—

He really meant that, it seemed, and he hoped Joanna would come down on the Friday evening.

'There's just one thing, Mr. Wilmore,' she began. But when his courteous voice said, 'Yes?' she lost her nerve and just added some triviality about not having any very formal evening wear.

'My dear child, that won't be at all necessary!' he assured her. 'It will be an entirely informal week-end. When the Warrenders come here they like to relax completely. I can't even promise that he will agree to hear you sing, though I have some hopes of persuading him to do so.'

'Oh – oh, thank you,' gasped Joanna, as fresh vistas of delight and terror opened out before her. Then she rang off and said, breathlessly, to her mother, 'It's all arranged.'

She worked very hard during the next few days. But she was not entirely happy with her singing lessons, for her substitute teacher showed little interest in her. Indeed, since Martha Singleton, the other Fiora, happened to be his star pupil, it was perhaps understandable that he found Joanna of secondary importance.

What did make her very happy was that when the reviews of the new play came out on Thursday morning, they were uniformly good.

'We must go!' her mother declared, forgetting her hard feelings against Elliot Cheam. And Joanna made it her business to go to the theatre during her lunchtime, where, however, she found a good many others had had the same idea, and there was a long line of people already waiting.

At the end of twenty minutes she had almost reached the box office when a side door swung open and out came Elliot Cheam. Overcome by inexplicable shyness, she would have let him pass without a sign. But he suddenly pulled up beside her and exclaimed, 'Hello! What are you doing, queueing for tickets?'

'The same as everyone else.' She smiled back at him. 'Waiting my turn, of course.'

'Nonsense. I'll see you have tickets.' He took her arm lightly and drew her away from the queue. 'When do you want to go?'

'But I couldn't let you – I mean, I've no special claim.'

'Of course you have. You brought us luck at the dress rehearsal, didn't you? *and* gave us our first good notice.' He grinned and took out a notebook. 'What evening?'

'Well, Mother and I thought Monday night might be less crowded.'

'You really are the perfect member of the public, aren't you?' He laughed outright as he scribbled down something in his book. 'Ask at the box office fifteen minutes before curtain time on Monday. The tickets will be there in your name.'

'Thank you *very* much. And, Mr. Cheam—'

'Elliot is the name.'

'Elliot, then. There's something I must tell you—'

'Mr. Cheam—' someone looked out of the box office – 'you're wanted on the phone in your office. Call from New York.'

Most of the waiting people turned an interested glance on Mr. Cheam at this arresting piece of information, and even Joanna was included in this scrutiny since he patted her arm as he said,

'All right. Enjoy yourself on Monday.' Then, with a quick smile, he went back through the side door, leaving her pretty sure that he had not even heard her last words.

It was possible, she told herself, that she might catch a glimpse of him on Monday evening, when she would insist on telling him that she was, after all, going to Wilmore Manor on the express (and unsolicited) invitation of his uncle. But when Monday evening came, although the tickets were waiting at the box office as promised, there was no sign of Elliot in the front of the house.

The seats were excellent ones, and her mother relented still further in her judgment of the producer. Indeed, when he and the author finally joined the cast for the last curtain, she whispered, 'Is he that very good-looking young man, or the one with the thinning hair?'

'He's the good-looking one. If you would call him good-looking,' added Joanna judicially.

'Most women would,' replied her mother simply.

Joanna wondered if she could summon enough courage to go round backstage, to thank him for the tickets and introduce her mother. But when they came out of the theatre it was raining hard and, by great good luck, a taxi drew up just in front of them.

'Jump in, darling,' her mother exclaimed. 'We can allow ourselves the luxury of a taxi home, considering the tickets were given to us.'

So they drove off, and Joanna decided she would write to Elliot, somehow embodying in her letter of thanks the casual information that she was going to the Manor at the week-end, after all. But it was all much too difficult when she came to the point. So, finally abandoning the attempt, she telephoned instead.

A pleasant female voice answered from Elliot Cheam's office. And when Joanna asked if she might speak to him, the female voice said – in the manner of all secretaries stalling on behalf of a busy boss – that Mr. Cheam had just gone out and she really didn't know when he might return, but could she do anything?

Joanna gave up further attempts at that point, merely leaving her name and asking that her thanks should be conveyed to Mr. Cheam for the tickets, with the added information that she and her mother had greatly enjoyed the performance.

'I'll be sure to tell him,' the pleasant voice promised. And there the matter rested.

'I've done all I can,' Joanna told herself defensively. 'Now I'm just going to enjoy my week-end – and explain about it later.'

And with this decision made, she suddenly found that she could look forward to the week-end visit with an almost tranquil mind.

She travelled down by train this time, since Mr. Wilmore had told her she would be met by car at the nearest station, about three miles from the Manor. She had assumed that the car would be a hired one, or chauffeur-driven, but as she came out of the charming little country station she saw Mr. Wilmore himself waiting for her.

This added the last drop to her cup of happiness and, on the short drive to the Manor, she chattered eagerly to him, telling him – among other things – about the success of his nephew's production and how much she and her mother had enjoyed the performance.

'I saw the notices were good,' he agreed. 'I had hoped Elliot might have come down this week-end, but I gather he'll be too busy. It's a pity.'

Joanna said, 'Yes,' not very truthfully, and then changed the subject to her own rehearsals for 'The Love of Three Kings'.

He was amused and pleased, she saw, to hear that she had been praised for her insight into the part of Fiora, and asked with genuine interest how her singing studies were going. She explained ruefully about the enforced change of teacher, and he looked grave about that, particularly when she added that this situation might well last until after the performances.

'And you don't like your present teacher?' he asked with concern.

'I don't *dis*like him,' Joanna explained quickly, 'only we don't seem to be on each other's wavelength, if I can put it that way.'

'It's a very good way to put it,' he said with a slight frown, 'and describes a rather serious situation. In my experience, unless there is personal rapport between student and teacher, the instruction is largely useless. We must see what can be done about this. Particularly with such an important performance coming up. Given reasonably good fortune, you might make quite a sensation as Fiora. And these things can count very much when one is first trying to attract attention.'

'I don't think,' Joanna told him diffidently, 'that anything *can* be done about it at the moment. Most of the vocal staff at the College are very much committed with their own work, naturally. I was lucky, I suppose, that someone could take me at all.'

'There is such a thing as private coaching,' replied her host, and he set his pleasant mouth with unusual firmness.

'Oh, but that can be terribly expensive! and my grant probably wouldn't apply there,' she said. 'I shall manage all right. It's unfortunate Miss Drayfield should be away at this particular point. But one has to accept these crises in any career, I suppose,' She sighed, slightly.

'Not necessarily,' he replied. 'Not if one has friends who are interested.'

And then they arrived at the Manor, and a few minutes later Joanna was being conducted upstairs by Mrs. Trimble and into the room she already thought of affectionately as *hers*.

'How lovely it all looks!' She glanced round contentedly. 'And how nice to see you again, Mrs. Trimble. You were so kind to me last time, and helped to make it such a memorable occasion.'

'I hope this will be another memorable occasion, Miss Joanna.' The housekeeper smiled, and Joanna was not unaware of the significant change in the form of address. 'Just come down when you're ready. Dinner is at eight, but I expect you would like a sherry with Mr. Wilmore first. Sir Oscar and Lady Warrender are not arriving until much later. They had to dine in town.'

So Joanna was able to relax and just enjoy the evening with her charming host, without feeling keyed up to make a good impression on the famous couple who were to share her week-end.

It was quite late in the evening when Mr. Wilmore said, 'Do you realize I haven't actually heard you sing yet? You look and move and even sometimes laugh in a way that reminds me irresistibly of Emilia. But what about the voice, I wonder?'

'Mr. Wilmore, please don't think of me in the Trangoni class,' Joanna said earnestly. 'She reached international standard even in her short career. I don't make any pretensions—'

'I know you don't. But – will you sing for me?'

'Of course, if you would like me to!' Joanna went

over to the piano immediately.

'Shall I play for you?' he asked unexpectedly.

'Please do – if you would be so kind.' She had already seen the vocal score of 'The Love of Three Kings' on the piano. 'You want me to sing something from this?'

'I should like that very much. From the first act?' he suggested. And when Joanna nodded he flicked over the pages and then began to play the long introduction to one of Fiora's most beautiful passages.

He played well, she noticed, with great feeling for the work, which was understandable in the circumstances. And she on her side tried to put into her singing all the subtle understanding of the role which her contact with him had given to her. Hers was not an outstandingly big voice, but she used it well, and the way she had begun to identify herself with Fiora helped her to give great poignancy and warmth to her interpretation.

Again it was perhaps inevitable that he should find a moving parallel between Joanna and the girl with whom he so personally associated the part. There was not very much lighting in the room, and most of what there was was concentrated over the piano. Joanna was rather in shadow and because she was a good actress – very much better that she herself had any idea – the result was quite stunning.

'It's almost unbelievable!' he exclaimed, his voice slightly unsteady with excitement and pleasure. 'Even the voice is similar, in some strange way. My dear child, you have no idea how much pleasure you have given me! And, in return, if any special coaching is needed for the perfecting of the role— Well, we'll talk of that later,' he said, breaking off sharply, as there were unmistakable sounds of the Warrenders arriving.

They came in like beings from another world, Joanna could not help thinking, their strong, clearly-defined personalities contrasting in the most extraordinary way with the half dreamlike scene which Justin Wilmore and she had created out of music and memories and the overall impression of the girl who had been in this house over thirty years ago.

Both the Warrenders seemed to remember her with some pleasure. At any rate, Anthea certainly did, and her famous husband went satisfactorily through the motions of appearing to do so, though Joanna thought she detected a certain degree of indifference beneath the surface. She did not hold it against him if that were the case. After all, she was pretty small fry in the Warrender world, and she was, as she knew, remarkably lucky to be there at all.

It was all very charming and enjoyable and, for Joanna at any rate, exciting. And when she finally went to bed in her already much-loved room, she felt that the week-end had made a wonderful beginning.

As she reflected on the scene just before the Warrenders' arrival, she tried to decide how much of Justin Wilmore's praise had been due to her actual gifts, and how much to the way she reminded him of what had obviously been the dearest person in his life. At any rate, she was glad the Warrenders had come in before he could say more about special coaching for her. There were limits to what one could accept from even the kindest of new friends.

The next day provided, as Mr. Wilmore had promised, a delightful degree of relaxation. They all spent a good deal of time in the beautiful garden, for although

71

it was October, the day was exceptionally fine and sunny. Much of the conversation, as might be expected, concerned the musical world, and Joanna listened eagerly and, without putting herself forward, tried to make sensible and reasonably knowledgeable replies when actually drawn into the discussion.

She left it to her host to speak about her own talents, only modifying his praise with a few murmurs of protest. But when Oscar Warrender said, 'We must hear you some time this evening,' she thought he really meant it, and that his rather alarming glance rested on her for a moment with a touch of genuine interest.

It was Anthea who said to her during the afternoon, 'It's rather touching and lovely that you should please Justin so much in the role of Fiora. Trangoni was his favourite artist – in fact, I think he was going to marry her when she was killed, poor girl – and she was specially associated with that role.'

'Yes, so he told me. It – troubles me a little, as well as pleasing me, as a matter of fact.'

'Why?' Anthea gave her a quick, inquiring glance.

'He seems to find quite a striking likeness between her and me, and last night, just before you arrived, I sang for him and he said even the voices were alike. I'm flattered, in a way, and only too pleased if it makes him happy. But I can't help thinking that perhaps his judgment of me as an artist is coloured by a certain amount of charming nostalgia.'

'Would it matter?' Anthea looked reflective. 'I mean if it's just a question of giving him pleasure.'

'Yes, I think it would. For one thing, one doesn't want to be just a shadow of someone else—'

'Oh, of course not.'

'And secondly, though I'm deeply grateful for his interest, I should be embarrassed if he assessed me far beyond my real talents and wanted to put me forward in that light. To anyone like Sir Oscar, for instance.'

'Yes, I see. Though you're being unusually modest for anyone in our profession,' Anthea said with a laugh. 'At least you needn't worry so far as my husband is concerned. He's never influenced by anyone else's opinion beforehand. If he hears you – and I'm sure he means to – you'll get the exact truth. Whether you want it or not, I'm afraid,' she added with a warning smile.

'I wouldn't want anything else,' Joanna declared earnestly. 'I was only thinking that he might well feel he was being asked to waste his time.'

'Oh, no!' Anthea was emphatic about that. 'He's always interested in voices. As he says, the fascinating thing is that one never knows where God will put a voice. Oscar found *me* in a rather stupid contest in a provincial town,' she added with a reminiscent smile.

'Did he?' Joanna looked intrigued. 'And was he thrilled?'

'If so, he concealed the fact at first,' Anthea said ruefully. 'He turned me down flat, in favour of another girl, who was very gifted though without a really fine voice.'

'You mean he didn't *recognize* your potential?' Joanna was shocked.

'Oh, yes, of course he did. He's a wizard in these matters. But he decided on the instant that a little easy success in the beginning would probably ruin me. So he saw to it that I lost the prize, and later arranged – in a rather devious way, I must admit – that he should

73

himself take over my training.'

'Wasn't that a ruthless way of doing things?' Joanna sounded slightly disapproving.

'Yes, of course,' Anthea agreed. 'But then Oscar *is* ruthless,' she added cheerfully. 'That's partly why he's a great musical director, I suppose.'

'I see,' said Joanna soberly. And presently she slipped away to her room and did a little anxious practising on her own. If she were to perform for the ruthless Sir Oscar, she had better see that at least she was in good voice.

The great moment came in the early evening, when they had all gathered in the drawing-room about an hour before dinner, and Warrender said abruptly, 'I'd like to hear you now, Miss Joanna. What are you going to sing for me?'

'She must sing some of Fiora's music,' put in Mr. Wilmore quickly.

'No. She can do so later.' The conductor was pleasant but firm. 'We'll have a little pure singing first. Do you sing any Mozart?'

'Pa-Pamina,' suggested Joanna timidly.

'Come, Pamina's music is a good enough test,' said Warrender amusedly and sat down at the piano. ' "*Ach, ich fuhls*"?'

Joanna nodded.

'Don't be frightened. Come and stand in the curve of the piano where I can see you,' ordered Warrender, as he had to many a scared performer before. 'Take your time, and think just what the words mean.'

She did as she was told and, nervous though she was, she felt somehow comforted by the commanding little smile that the conductor gave her just as she made her entry. To her surprise, it was all distinctly easier than

74

she had feared. She kept her eyes on him most of the time and, by the slightest glance or movement of his hand, he conveyed to her what it was she should be doing.

'Um-hm,' he said, non-committally but not discouragingly, at the end. 'Now let's hear what you've been doing with Fiora.'

This was familiar ground for Joanna – temperamentally suited to her, carefully and lovingly studied, and of very personal interest. Insensibly she relaxed and, after the first two bars, she was back in the identity of the tragic character which so deeply fascinated her. She no longer stood rigidly in the curve of the piano, though her slight movements were economical and of unfailing significance, while her mobile face became even more expressive than the phrases she was singing.

She was lost in the part, unaware of the people around her, or of the slight stir in the hall of someone arriving. As Warrender ceased playing, she closed her eyes for a moment and then opened them again, like someone coming out of a half-sleep. Then she looked across at the conductor.

'You want the exact truth, I take it?' he said, leaning back and regarding her with some interest.

'Of – of course.'

'Not "of course" at all,' Warrender assured her. 'Few people want the exact truth, unless it coincides with what they hope to hear. But I am going to tell you right away – you have not got what is called a great voice. I'm not even sure you have an operatic voice at all. On the other hand—'

He paused, for at that moment the drawing-room door opened, and into the room came Elliot Cheam.

75

CHAPTER FOUR

'My dear boy! What a delightful surprise!'

Mr. Wilmore's pleasure and astonishment were such that he accepted even this interruption to Oscar Warrender's pronouncement with equanimity. And both the conductor and his wife were also undeniably pleased at Elliot Cheam's unexpected appearance.

Only Joanna, standing wordless by the piano, was frozen into a sort of rigid dismay. She had not even had time to recover from the shock of Warrender's verdict – or receive whatever comfort might follow his words 'on the other hand' – before the very thing she had most dreaded was upon her, like something in a bad dream.

Here she was, a guest in his uncle's house, after she had protested to Elliot with such vehemence that nothing was further from her intentions than to get herself invited to Wilmore Manor while the Warrenders were there.

As for Elliot, it was plain from his expression what he was thinking. He greeted his uncle and the Warrenders with easy friendliness, explaining how he had unexpectedly managed to be free from his theatre commitments, and then paused for a moment before Joanna. With a smile which chilled her heart but made her cheeks hot, he said lightly, 'I thought perhaps I might find you here.'

Then, before anything else could be said, the manservant appeared at the door and announced that dinner was served.

'Come, you couldn't have arrived at a better moment,

Elliot.' His uncle clapped him affectionately on the shoulder. 'Over dinner you must tell us all about your first night. And we must also hear what Warrender has to say about Joanna, who has just been singing to us.'

'I thought he had already pronounced,' replied Elliot dryly as they went into the dining-room. 'Didn't I hear something about hers not being an operatic voice, as I came in?'

'That statement, unqualified, would not be the whole truth,' said the conductor, as they took their seats at the round, candle-lit table. 'I'm sorry the interruption came just when it did, for I must have left Miss Joanna feeling somewhat dashed.'

'It's all right.' Somehow Joanna fought down her terrible disappointment as well as her shock over Elliot's arrival, and even managed to give the conductor an unsteady smile. 'I never had very exaggerated notions of my gifts. It was just—'

'That you felt, given the right boost, you might make it?' suggested Elliot smoothly. The words themselves were inoffensive, and Joanna doubted if anyone else at the table knew that they carried a special sting. But *she* knew what he meant, and she felt as though he had slapped her in the face.

Then unexpectedly Anthea Warrender spoke, and her clear, sweet but somehow authoritative voice carried a sound of rescue to Joanna's ears.

'Could we please hear *all* of what Oscar was going to say?' she suggested. 'As a singer myself, I sympathize very much with Joanna, who's heard only the more critical half of the verdict so far.'

'Certainly let us have the sugar on the pill,' agreed Elliot. But this time he had gone too far.

'Stop making snide remarks, Elliot Cheam,' said Anthea crisply and, Joanna noted with some satisfaction, he then looked a little as though *his* face had been slapped. 'If you're sore because your play isn't the number one topic, you might remember that it was Joanna who encouraged you and boosted *your* morale, just before the first night of your play.'

'My apologies,' murmured Elliot, a good deal startled, while Warrender looked amused at his wife's determination to clear the decks for whatever he had to say.

'Thank you.' He gave Anthea a slight, mocking bow. And the implication that it was his interests rather than hers that were being taken care of steadied Joanna a little. 'As I said – and as you probably sense yourself – yours is not a great voice of unique quality. More a good instrument, musically and intelligently used. With luck – on which none of us can count – you might make an operatic career. But I would not care to bank on that. What you have got, however, unless I'm much mistaken, is a quite remarkable dramatic talent. She should interest you, Elliot—' he turned suddenly to Cheam, who was studying the wine in his glass, as though the discussion held no interest for him.

Elliot glanced up.

'I'm not looking for new dramatic talent at the moment,' he stated coolly.

'No?' Warrender smiled dryly. 'When you get to my age you'll realize one looks humbly for real talent all the time.'

'Well, of course—' Elliot was slightly taken aback. 'But in this case—'

He left the sentence unfinished, as though that in itself should express his opinion. But Warrender was too old a hand to accept an answer that lacked clear definition.

'In this case—?' he repeated, and Elliot shifted slightly and frowned.

'My dear Warrender, I cannot help wondering what opportunity you can have had to test Miss Ransome's dramatic talent. She has sung to you – in a drawing-room, quite informally. I would accept your musical judgment anywhere, of course, in any circum-stances—'

'Too kind of you,' interjected Warrender disagree-ably.

'—but so far as her theatrical abilities are concerned—'

'I am not without theatrical experience either,' said Oscar Warrender with deceptive mildness. 'I merely suggest—'

'Please!' Choking with embarrassment and the difficulty of controlling her tears, Joanna interrupted almost fiercely. 'Can't we change the subject? It's dreadful to be the cause of an argument across Mr. Wilmore's dinner table. I mean – I mean—'

'You mean it almost makes you wish you weren't here.' Elliot smiled dangerously at her. 'Let us change the subject, by all means.' And he began to talk about the first night of his new production, so entertainingly and amusingly that the tension relaxed immediately.

Even Joanna managed to contribute her quota of smiling interest. Though no one – except perhaps Elliot Cheam – could have guessed what the effort cost her. The dramatic talent with which Oscar Warrender had credited her would never be more sorely needed, she thought desperately, than it was needed that evening.

It was over at last, that dinner which anyone might have envied her, that evening which should have been an opera-lover's dream. She had managed to make her host believe she was really enjoying herself; she had concealed from the Warrenders that his verdict had dealt a mortal blow to her fondest hopes; and, above all, she hoped and believed she had convinced Elliot Cheam that she cared less than nothing about anything he might think of her.

When at last bedtime came and she felt she could make her retreat, she bade everyone a charming good night and went out of the room, her dignity and self-respect still almost intact.

She was half-way up the stairs when she realized that she had left her favourite scarf behind her, and reluctantly she went back. As she reached the drawing-room door, however, she heard Mr. Wilmore say,

'She's a brave girl, but I'm afraid she was desperately disappointed, though she put a good face on it. I wonder if perhaps, with extra coaching of some sort—'

'She's a tough little cookie, as a matter of fact, under that dewy-eyed exterior,' his nephew cut in. 'If you want my opinion—'

And then Joanna fled back up the stairs, willing to lose her scarf for ever, rather than listen to any more discussion about herself. Tough little cookie, indeed! Vulgar, horrid, ill-wishing beast that he was!

She flung herself on the bed and wept – the hot, heartbreaking tears she had kept back all the evening. Without Elliot Cheam to add his odious, disparaging comments and contemptuous glances, she thought she could have borne the crushing disappointment of Oscar Warrender's verdict. He had given it not unkindly, and she had assured him beforehand that she wanted the absolute truth.

She still wanted the truth, she supposed, for what

was the good of trying to found a musical career – or any other career, come to that – on something less? Better accept the true position rather than wander on in a fool's paradise.

Even so, she did ask herself if it were remotely possible that Warrender could be mistaken. Or could it be that, just as with Anthea in her early days, he thought for some reason that a harsh judgment might be healthy at this early stage?

She toyed with these two possibilities for a few moments. But only a few. Such a theory would not stand up to any sensible examination. Warrender had no conceivable reason to tell her anything but what he judged to be the truth. And, as for the possibility of his being mistaken in his judgment, where was she likely to find a more informed or reliable verdict than his?

Strangely enough, she even thought as she tossed uneasily on the bed that deep down inside her his measured words rang a sort of bell. She loved singing, she was perfectionist enough to want to develop her gifts to the highest point. But hers was *not* one of those glorious, memorable organs that made musical history. Warrender was right there.

Given luck – or, to use Elliot Cheam's horrid expression, the right boost—

She winced away from that wording. Innocent though it might be as applied to most people, *he* had applied it to her in the sense that she had been trying to cadge a lift on the road to success from his unsuspecting uncle.

Joanna had stopped crying by now, only an occasional after-sob shaking her from time to time. And at last she began to think of the few words of consolation Oscar Warrender had felt able to give her. She had considerable dramatic talent, in his opinion.

Well, it was true that the drama behind what she was singing had always fascinated her. It was the portrayal of a character like Fiora which had brought out all the best in her work. But, for all practical purposes, how did that help her?

Not at all, so far as Elliot Cheam was concerned. His contemptuous dismissal of Warrender's attempt to interest him rankled more than anything else in the whole evening. For Elliot, alas, was the real theatrical expert in the party.

Oscar Warrender might say she had theatrical talent, as Elliot might say of someone that the voice was noteworthy. In each case it would be an informed opinion from someone who had links with the other man's world. But it would not be the final expert judgment on which one might build hopes of a career.

She was not prepared to leave it at that, of course. She was determined to go on with her studies for the moment. Let her see what the performance of 'The Love of Three Kings' might do for her. But it was useless to pretend that her drive and hopeful determination had not received a fearful check.

At no point did she blame Oscar Warrender as over-ruthless. She had asked for his informed opinion — probably the best informed opinion in the operatic world. A man of integrity — and no one had ever questioned Warrender's integrity, whatever else they might say of him — could do no less than tell her the truth as he saw it. It was not his fault that the verdict had been given at just about the worst moment in time for poor Joanna.

She fell asleep at last, slept dreamlessly and woke to a wonderful morning and a feeling of deepest depression. It was a moment before she realized why her heart was so heavy. Then all the events of the previous evening rushed back upon her, and she wanted nothing so much as to put her head under the bedclothes and refuse to face the day.

Rejecting this cowardly impulse, however, she got up, bathed and dressed and then went downstairs through the still almost silent house. A few sounds were coming from the kitchen regions, but no one else seemed awake in the rest of the house. So she went out on to the terrace and then down the few steps to a charming walled garden, where tall yew hedges gave an air of privacy to the several pathways.

The faint mist of a warm October morning had already almost lifted, and the scent of late roses was incredibly sweet. It was also a trifle melancholy to anyone in Joanna's present mood, for it seemed to speak irresistibly of the passing of the joys of high summer.

'Oh, stop being so fanciful and self-pitying!' she told herself, actually speaking aloud. Then she turned a corner and came upon Elliot Cheam.

He was standing by an ornamental stone wall, making overtures to a superior-looking black Persian cat who was totally ignoring him.

'Hello—' he turned to look at Joanna – 'were you addressing me?'

'No.' She hoped he had not heard her exact words. 'I was – talking to myself, I'm afraid.'

'Well, I was talking to this unresponsive cat, which is only one degree better, I suppose. His complete indifference is very chastening. – Oh!' he added sharply as the cat, unerringly sensing a decrease in interest, put out a paw and dabbed him lightly on the cheek.

Joanna laughed outright and said impulsively, 'It must be a she. She didn't like being ignored.'

'You think so?' He laughed too and then looked slightly surprised to find that he had done so. 'Is that the way it works?' And he turned back to stroke the cat, who immediately rubbed its head against his hand with an entirely spurious air of slavish affection.

'It works with some women and most cats,' Joanna assured him. And then – she simply could not imagine why – she added, 'It would work with Sara Fernie, I expect.'

'What makes you say that, I wonder?' He abandoned the cat – who instantly assumed an air of indifference once more – and fell into step beside Joanna.

'I don't really know,' she exclaimed. 'And *I* was being rather catty even to say it, I suppose. She means a lot to you, doesn't she?'

'Our careers have been very closely linked for some time,' he agreed. 'And most of that time I've thought myself in love with her,' he added with startling candour.

'But don't you *know* whether you're in love with her or not?'

'No,' he said lightly. 'Does one ever?'

'Well, I should have thought one did,' replied Joanna, in the tone she used when her mother was being silly. 'But that's not an expert opinion. I've never been in love.'

'Haven't you?' He glanced at her with amused interest. 'Just devoted to your career, to the exclusion of all else, I take it?'

'Not to the exclusion of all else,' she replied steadily. 'And if you're preparing to be unpleasant again about

84

my being down here at Wilmore Manor when I had told you I had no intention of coming—'

'When you had gone to absurd lengths to assure me you wouldn't dream of coming,' he corrected smoothly.

'I did not go to any absurd lengths!' She kept her temper firmly in check. 'When I was speaking to you I told the exact truth, as it was at that moment. I had no intention of coming here this week-end. For one thing, I hadn't been invited, and—'

'A mere formality, surely, when you'd been so busy charming my uncle?'

'Am I telling this story, or are you?' she asked, so crisply that he glanced at her in surprise. 'And why, incidentally, were *you* at such pains to tell *me* you couldn't come down here, when all the time you meant to come sneaking down to see if I were here?'

'I did nothing of the sort!' He was suddenly furious. 'How dare you suggest—?'

'It's horrid when people make stupid and unfounded accusations, isn't it?' she said sweetly, and there was a long silence.

'You're saying—' he spoke slowly and reluctantly at last – 'that my accusations are stupid and unfounded?'

'I'm saying just that,' she agreed, but there was no bitterness in her tone now and, after a moment, she took him by the arm, which seemed to surprise him a good deal. 'Elliot – you said at a kinder moment that I might call you Elliot, although I noticed last night that you studiously referred to me as Miss Ransome—'

'I'm sorry about that. It was silly,' he said unexpectedly.

'Well, it was rather,' she agreed goodhumouredly,

'but we'll forget that. What's more important is – why did you decide to dislike me, from the moment I first entered your uncle's house?'

'I didn't!' he protested defensively.

'You did, you know. You made up your mind that I was out to exploit your uncle in some shameful and idiotic way, and ever since then you've been busy fitting everything else into your theory. I don't happen to mind much what you think—'

'Don't you?' he said unexpectedly, and the single question almost stopped her breath for a moment, because something deep down in her instantly registered the conviction that her assertion was a lie.

'Of course I don't,' she declared lightly. 'Why should I? Except that no one likes to be misjudged all the time. I genuinely like and admire your uncle; I was touched that he took a personal interest in me, even though that interest was founded on his regard for someone else long ago; and when he phoned – entirely on his own initiative, I might say – I couldn't really see why I shouldn't accept. Can you?'

'You might at least have mentioned it to me, surely? After jumping down my throat at the very suggestion that you might be thinking of going, I mean.'

'I did try to tell you. I made an attempt that time you found me at the box office and were so kind as to offer me t-tickets for your show.' Her voice shook slightly as she remembered what a happy moment that had been. 'But before I could do so you were called away and—'

'Called away?' He sounded sceptical again.

'It was a transatlantic telephone call, and I couldn't very well insist on detaining you.'

'Oh—' she saw he recalled the occasion exactly. 'But

surely—' he gave the impression of being reluctantly driven from one line of defence to another – 'surely there were other times when you could have told me – asked me—' he stopped.

'You mean you really feel that I was wrong to accept your uncle's invitation without asking your permission first?'

'No, of course not.' He looked quite outraged at that suggestion.

'What, then?' she asked, in her most reasonable tone.

'Oh, I don't know.' He frowned and then laughed angrily. 'You're trying to make me feel a fool, aren't you?'

'No,' she said. And then, when they had walked on a few paces, she added, 'But if you *are* feeling a bit of a fool, who am I to argue with you about it?'

He laughed reluctantly at that and exclaimed, 'All right, you win. What do you want me to do? Apologize abjectly?'

'No, of course not.' It was she who was outraged that time. 'What a horrible idea!'

'Think so?' He gave her an amused, speculative glance. 'I thought that was what most women liked, once they'd won their point.'

'Not most women,' she assured him firmly. 'Perhaps the Sara Fernies of this world might.'

'You *have* got a down on Sara, haven't you?' he said amusedly.

'No, I haven't. She's no business of mine. But I was shocked at some of the things she said at that dress rehearsal.'

'Were you? What, for instance?' He looked genuinely curious.

'Never mind now. But, if you're really keen on her,

you'd better show her a touch of healthy indifference from time to time. Like the cat on the wall, you know.'

'She's coming over here this afternoon,' he said irrelevantly. 'At least, I expect she is.'

'Is she?' Joanna looked surprised. 'Did she also come down from London last night, then?'

'No, no. She had to be there for the evening performance, of course. But we – disagreed about something. Well, she wanted me to hang about last night and then drive her down here this morning. Whereas—'

'You couldn't wait to get here and find out whether I'd stolen a march on you or not,' suggested Joanna.

'Not at all,' he replied stiffly. 'It had nothing to do with you at all. In fact, until I actually saw you there in the drawing-room I hadn't thought again about our conversation.'

'That wasn't the impression you gave.'

'Look here, I thought we'd agreed on a sort of peace pact,' he said protestingly.

'I'm sorry!' she laughed, but with a touch of genuine contrition. 'Go on about Sara. She was annoyed because you wouldn't wait for her and come down this morning.'

'Whereas I – who really could get away – looked forward to an evening with my uncle and the Warrenders. So I went. But I imagine she'll take the morning train down. She has a week-end cottage near here, you know.'

'Yes, I remember,' said Joanna, not adding – though she thought it – that no doubt this was a very useful way of keeping a hand on him. 'So I suppose,' she added after a moment, 'that you'll drive her back to town and all will once more be well.'

'For the time being,' he agreed rather moodily. Then a nearby church clock struck the half-hour and he said, 'That sounds like breakfast time. Shall we go in?'

They went towards the house together, Joanna reflecting, not without pleasure, on what he had said about a peace pact.

Well, at least she had had some opportunity to justify herself, and she felt quite amazingly happier because of that. Inevitably, Oscar Warrender's verdict on her voice lingered unhappily in the back of her consciousness. But somehow even that seemed less shattering when she reviewed her talk with Elliot Cheam in the garden.

He was quite right about Sara. Just before lunch she drifted in, looking absolutely lovely and displaying a deceptively soft and friendly mood. She knew the Warrenders slightly, it seemed, and they were all agreeable to each other, in the way people are when they have a certain amount of professional interests in common but no special personal rapport.

She seemed to have some difficulty in recalling who Joanna was, although Joanna did not doubt that she remembered perfectly their first meeting, and also the dress rehearsal which had ended with Elliot taking her out to dinner instead of Sara.

To Mr. Wilmore Sara was specially affectionate and even respectful, and twice she called him Uncle Justin, which Joanna privately thought excessive, especially when she recalled what Mrs. Trimble had said. Elliot, however, seemed to find nothing remarkable in it, and Joanna reminded herself that it was really not at all her business how any of these people chose to address each other.

During the afternoon the Warrenders went with their host to see some recent additions to his famous collection. Joanna would really have liked to go too, but no one made the suggestion. And, feeling considerably less than a professional after what had happened last night, she hardly liked to make the suggestion herself, lest she should find herself something of an intruder in a conversation between experts.

So she stayed in the long drawing-room, occupying herself quite happily with a splendid musical reference book which she had never had a chance to examine before. She was deep in this when she realized from approaching voices that Elliot and Sara were crossing the hall towards the room where she was. Her instinct was to escape and leave them the place to themselves. But she had only just reached one of the french windows which opened on to the terrace when they came in.

To depart now would look too self-consciously like flight, so she paused by the window, as though looking out at the remarkably beautiful view, determined that in a few minutes she would make good her escape.

The other two were speaking of their play and Elliot, catching sight of Joanna said, 'Joanna went during the second week and tells me she thought you brilliant, Sara.'

'Really?' Sara's slight smile was no more than a conventional flick of attention in Joanna's direction. 'How did you like the play itself?'

'Enormously,' Joanna said sincerely. 'I imagine it's in for a long run, isn't it?'

'We hope so,' observed Elliot.

'I think I hope so,' amended Sara.

'Doesn't one always hope for a long run?' Joanna looked surprised.

'Oh, in a way – of course.' Sara shrugged. 'It's what one prays for on the first night. But the moment you've settled down to it you realize afresh what a ruthless tie it is. Every single night except Sunday gone for heaven knows how long. It's penal servitude if you're one of the principals. For the producer it's not so bad.' She glanced across at Elliot under her long lashes. 'He can get away, once the whole thing is running smoothly. But for the cast, particularly in the early part of the run, there's no let-up. The public don't take kindly to understudies.'

'Point taken,' said Elliot, sliding down a little further in his chair and grinning across at Sara in a slightly placatory way.

'Well—' she laughed charmingly – 'now you know why I felt deserted last night. But you're forgiven. I take it we're driving back to town together tonight – or tomorrow morning.'

'Cat on the wall,' said Joanna quite distinctly, as she stared out of the window with apparent concentration.

'What?' Sara glanced over at her, surprised and not too pleased at this interruption.

'The cat we saw on the wall this morning, Elliot – remember?' Joanna flashed him a quick smile.

'What about it?' he asked defensively. But he got up and came over to where she was standing.

'It ran across the lawn just a moment ago,' lied Joanna smoothly.

'Who cares about a stupid cat?' exclaimed Sara in the room behind them. 'I said – I suppose you're driving me back to town, Elliot?'

There was an infinitesimal pause and then Elliot said deliberately, 'I'm sorry, my dear, I've already prom-

91

ised to drive Joanna home. And as you know, three makes rather a crush in my car.'

Sara was the last woman in the world to submit to being a crushed third in anyone's car. She gave a slight laugh which, however, to Joanna's ears, carried a faintly startled note.

'That's all right,' she said coolly. 'I'll take the morning train back. It's quicker anyway, and will give me at least one peaceful, relaxed night in the country. You're going back tonight, I take it?'

Again that tiny pause. But this time, Joanna realized, Elliot was in the dilemma of not knowing what her plans really were. So she answered quite sweetly and firmly for him – 'Yes, we're going back tonight.'

'After dinner,' Elliot amended.

'I see.' Sara sounded goodhumoured indifference personified. But just for a second she gave Joanna the kind of glance a Borgia might have given when measuring the next victim for a poisoned ring.

'Too stupid of me to get myself involved in this,' Joanna told herself, as she strolled out on to the terrace and down to the garden. 'What are they to me, anyway? Except that he's too nice to be a meal for a man-eating tigress. At least, I suppose he is.'

Later, when she was putting the few last things into her case before going down to dinner, Mrs. Trimble came to ask if she would be catching a train or a bus back to town, as the Sunday timetables might not be familiar to her.

'Neither, Mrs. Trimble. I'm being really spoiled, instead,' Joanna explained. 'Mr. Cheam has very kindly offered to give me a lift back to town.'

'Has he, now?' Mrs. Trimble looked interested, and even a trifle amused. 'But he hasn't got his bigger car with him, has he?'

'I don't think he can have,' replied Joanna demurely. 'He told Miss Fernie it only took two comfortably.'

'Well, well,' said the housekeeper. And it occurred to Joanna that a surprising amount of significance, not to say satisfaction, could be crammed into that simple repetition.

Sara stayed to dinner, giving very much the impression that she was virtually a member of the family and assuming – quite correctly, as a matter of fact – that Mr. Wilmore would drive her over to her own place when his guests had departed. The Warrenders were leaving at the same time as Elliot and Joanna, though they were driving straight to their Thamesside home and not actually to London.

In the flurry of final good-byes, Joanna was touched and a little surprised to be kissed by Anthea, and not at all surprised to be more or less ignored by Sara. Mr. Wilmore bade her a very kind good-bye, telling her that he looked forward to her making other visits to the Manor, and adding that he intended to come to London to be present when she sang in 'The Love of Three Kings'.

'Oh—' with a conscious effort, Joanna gathered together something of her one-time enthusiasm about that event – 'I shall do my very best if I know you're there.'

'You will do your very best anyway,' said Oscar Warrender sternly behind her. 'No real artist must ever do less than that.'

'But of course.' She turned eagerly to speak to him. 'And, Mr. Warrender, though you had to tell me some unwelcome truths, I promise you it won't make me work any less hard for the performance.'

'I'm glad to hear that. I shall be there,' he added, almost as an afterthought.

'*You* will?' She gazed in astonishment at the great conductor. 'But why?'

'I happen to like the work,' he replied, in a tone which did not encourage further questions.

'Oh? – oh, yes, I see.'

She said good-bye then and went across to where Elliot was sitting in the driving seat of his car. She already had one foot on the step when suddenly a thought struck her, and she ran back impulsively to where the Warrenders were still exchanging a last few words with their host.

'Sir Oscar,' she said breathlessly, 'if you don't mind my telling you, I'm in the *second* cast.'

'I know.' He looked down at her from his considerable height. 'That's why I shall be at the second performance.'

'Oh—' she swallowed a great, excited lump in her throat – 'but you as good as said I wasn't interesting material.'

'No, I didn't say that at all. I said you had not got a great or memorable voice. I never said you did not interest me. On the contrary, it is just possible that you might interest me profoundly. But to decide that I should have to hear you – and see you – on a stage.'

'You mean—?'

'I'm not going to tell you what I mean,' stated Warrender unequivocally. 'There may be absolutely nothing in the idea I have. But, unlike our friend Elliot, I am prepared to follow my professional hunches wherever they may take me. Even,' he added a little distastefully, 'to a students' performance. Now run along,'

CHAPTER FIVE

OBEDIENT to the conductor's injunction, Joanna 'ran along'. Or rather, she walked slowly and not quite steadily across to the car and silently got in beside Elliot.

'What did Warrender say that gave you such a shock?' he wanted to know, as he started the car.

'It wasn't a shock,' said Joanna. 'At least, it was a very nice kind of shock. He said he would be coming to the performance. *My* performance! "The Love of Three Kings". And he said specifically the second performance, so that he could hear me.'

'But I thought you said it was more or less a students' performance.' Elliot sounded incredulous. 'I never heard of Oscar Warrender going to an end-of-term college show. He can't have been serious.'

'He was very serious.' Joanna was insistent on that. 'In fact, he said that, unlike you – his words, not mine – he was prepared to follow his professional hunches wherever they might take him. Even to a students' performance. What do you think he meant by that, quite?'

'I have no idea. But—' Elliot grinned suddenly – 'I begin to think I ought to come to this show too.'

'No, please don't. You'd make me nervous.'

'And won't Warrender make you nervous?'

'Not in the same way.'

He teased her a good deal about the way in which he made her nervous, but she refused to be drawn, and presently put an end to the subject by saying, 'I haven't

95

thanked you yet for giving me this lift home.'

'Shouldn't I be doing the thanking?' he countered. 'I thought I was the object of a rescue operation.'

Joanna laughed and said, 'It was just a spur-of-the-moment idea, really. If you didn't want to be rescued, I suppose you could have left the conversation at no more than a discussion about cats.'

'I was too much intrigued to do that,' he declared. 'I felt I must at least try out your theory. I'll let you know if it works.'

She was silent at that. On the one hand, she had no wish to be involved in any difficulty between Elliot and Sara, whom she judged to be dangerous; and, on the other, she found she very much liked the idea that Elliot intended to keep in touch.

They drove for some time without further conversation, but the silence was oddly companionable. Then Joanna said, 'You needn't drive me right home, you know. If you drop me at a convenient Tube station, I can quite easily—'

'I'm driving you right home,' he assured her. 'Where exactly is "home", by the way?'

She told him, and added, 'I live there with my mother.'

'Yes, I remember. You told me,' he said, and she felt disproportionately gratified that he had remembered that detail about her. 'You brought her with you to the theatre, didn't you? You should have come backstage with her and introduced us.'

'It was raining, otherwise I might have. But, if it interests you, she noticed you when you came on the stage with the author at the end.'

'Did she?' He looked gratified in his turn. 'What did she say?'

'She asked if you were the bald one—'

'Oh!'

'—or the good-looking one.'

'Come, that's better. And how did you answer that?' he inquired with interest.

'I said you were the good-looking one, if one would call you that.'

'That's a nasty crack.'

'And my mother said that most women would.'

'I like the sound of your mother,' he declared. 'Will it be too late to come in and meet her when we arrive?'

'I expect so,' said Joanna in her least encouraging tone.

But when they arrived at the small, pleasant house where Joanna and her mother lived, fate obligingly played into Elliot's hands. For Mrs. Ransome, looking extraordinarily pretty and appealing in the lamplight, came running out to lean her arms on the gate like someone in a charming, if slightly old-fashioned musical comedy.

'Hello, darling,' she called eagerly. 'Did you have a wonderful time?'

'Wonderful,' Joanna assured her. 'This is Mr. Elliot Cheam, Mother. You remember seeing him on the stage the other night.'

'I was the good-looking one, Mrs. Ransome, not the bald one,' Elliot amplified, smiling down at her. Whereat she fluttered her long eyelashes at him. And he was so delighted by this demonstration of an almost completely lost art that he exclaimed, 'Do that again!'

'Do what again?' Mrs. Ransome asked, while Joanne almost gaped to see this immediate rapport established between her charming, silly mother and the not very approachable Elliot.

'Flutter your eyelashes. The only other woman I know who can do that is my own mother,' Elliot explained. 'And it doesn't come naturally to her as it does to you.'

'Don't be silly,' said Mrs. Ransome, enchanted. 'Would you like to come in and have some coffee after your long drive?'

Elliot said he would love to, before Joanna could intervene. So they all went into the house where, in point of fact, Joanna made the coffee while her mother and Elliot Cheam discussed whether the old-fashioned feminine grace of the past were instinctive or carefully cultivated.

Over the coffee Mrs. Ransome noticed her daughter again and asked about her meeting with the Warrenders.

'Did you sing to him, dear? and what did he have to say?'

'I did sing to him,' Joanna admitted. 'And,' she added with grim accuracy, 'he said mine was not a great or memorable voice. Perhaps not even an operatic voice at all.'

'Stupid man,' said her mother, dismissing one of the greatest conductors of the day with splendid subjectivity. 'No need for you to think any more about him.'

'Joanna has to think about him,' put in Elliot firmly. 'He is coming to hear her in "The Love of Three Kings".'

'Why? if he can't appreciate her?' Mrs. Ransome asked.

'We don't know,' explained Elliot, as though he and

Joanna were as one in this. 'We find it most intri-
guing.'

'Probably he really thinks she *is* good, but is jealous
because she is better than his wife,' suggested Mrs.
Ransome, reducing both her daughter and Elliot
Cheam to momentary silence by this staggering
theory.

'I hardly think it could be that,' murmured Elliot
finally. While Joanna said indulgently, 'Don't be ridiculous, Mother. He said that in some way I interested
him. As an artist, of course,' she added hastily, before
her mother could put forward any further absurdity.
'But he wouldn't say in what way. He put it that he
would have to see me on a stage first, and that's why
he's coming to the performance.'

'A lot of mystery about nothing, it seems to me,'
declared her mother cheerfully. 'But I suppose if you
are Oscar Warrender you feel you should behave like
the Oracle of Wherever-it-was from time to time.
Anyway, we shall see for ourselves on the night, shan't
we?' She appealed smilingly to Elliot, who said re-
gretfully,

'I shan't, I'm afraid. Joanna says I can't come.'

'Nonsense! Of course you can come,' replied Mrs.
Ransome. '*I* invite you – and I shall expect you.'

'Mrs. Ransome,' said Elliot, getting up, 'if you
hadn't already made my evening by fluttering your
eyelashes at me, you would have made it now. I must
go, but thank you for the coffee, the welcome and the
invitation.'

Then he kissed Mrs. Ransome's hand with great
panache, said a more casual good night to Joanna and
took his leave.

'What a nice man!' Joanna's mother said when he

99

had gone. 'I don't know why you started by disliking him and criticizing him.'

'It's too long a story to recapitulate now.' Joanna smothered a yawn. 'But he did suggest a peace pact earlier today, and I admit I'm glad to be on good terms with him, after all. Do you really like him, Mother?'

'Yes, very much. Don't you?'

'I think—' Joanna smiled slowly – 'that perhaps I do. I didn't really mean him to come to the performance, and his being there will make me nervous. But somehow I'm glad you asked him.'

'I have a sort of instinct about these things,' declared her mother happily, and Joanna saw no reason why she should dispute this.

During the remaining three weeks before the performance she worked devotedly on the role of Fiora. Most of the time she managed to push into the back of her mind what Oscar Warrender had said about her voice not being an operatic one, and to remember only that, contrary to anything that anyone might have expected, he intended to be there on the great night because, in his own words, she 'interested him profoundly'.

Joanna herself breathed not a word at the College about the likelihood of the famous Warrender attending. But somehow some hint of it must have got out, because when she came to the final rehearsal, she found several of the cast in a state of what could only be described as blissful jitters.

'Have you heard?' Martha Singleton, the other Fiora, said to her. 'The rumour is going round that Sir Oscar Warrender will be coming to the first night.'

Just in time Joanna stopped herself from saying, 'No – the second night, I think,' and merely contented herself with asking where Martha had heard this story.

'Joyce Feldon got it from Dr. Evans's secretary. Apparently two tickets were sent to him, by request.'

'Perhaps,' suggested Joanna somewhat disingenuously, 'it's just a case of complimentary tickets being sent, whether he uses them or not.'

'No. They were sent by request. That means they were requested *by him*, I take it.'

'And Joyce was sure they were for the first night?'

'Why, of course. People like that always come to hear the first cast,' replied Martha with almost naïve self-confidence.

Joanna was generous enough to feel sorry that there was a disappointment in store for Martha. But she would have been superhuman if she had not exulted a little in her certainty that Warrender was not coming to hear Martha.

The first performance was, fortunately, a well-deserved success for most of the cast, and any disappointment that might have been engendered by the non-appearance of the famous conductor was swallowed up in the enthusiastic reception by the audience and the favourable notices which the performance received from the Press the next morning.

'Yes, very nice, dear,' said Joanna's mother when Joanna asked if she had read the notices. 'But of course everyone is really waiting for *tonight's* performance.'

'They aren't, you know,' Joanna felt bound to point out. 'It's usually the first performance which arouses most interest.'

'Then why is Oscar Warrender coming to the second performance?' inquired her mother, unanswerably. At which Joanna most illogically felt a queer sense of chill emptiness somewhere in the pit of her stomach at the frightful thought that perhaps he might change his mind and not bother, after all, to come to either performance.

Her sense of self-discipline, however, enabled her to ignore her fears and doubts for most of the day and to concentrate on doing her very best, whoever might come or not come. And she was cheered, as well as touched, to find on her arrival in her dressing-room that there, waiting for her, was a small but exquisite basket of flowers from Mr. Wilmore and some very handsome roses from Elliot Cheam.

'Somebody somewhere *remembered* you, as the flower-shop advertisements say,' observed a fellow student who had looked in to wish her luck. 'Who sent that lovely little basket of flowers? Very choice, I must say.'

'A friend of mine called Justin Wilmore. He has a famous—'

'*The* Justin Wilmore?'

'Yes, I suppose one could call him that.'

'He must be the distinguished-looking elderly man who arrived a few minutes ago with the Warrenders.'

'The – Warrenders?' Joanna gave a little gasp of mingled relief and alarm. 'They did come, then!'

'Yes. Didn't you know? Oh, perhaps I shouldn't have told you. Will it make you nervous?'

'Not more nervous than I am already,' replied Joanna with a shaky little laugh. And then her friend repeated her good wishes and left.

The last quarter of an hour before the rise of the curtain was, naturally, nerve-racking. But when the actual moment of her entry on the stage came Joanna conquered her sense of tension, recalled with almost loving tenderness the girl who had made this part so much her own, and told herself she would try to be a worthy, if humble, successor. From there she slipped instinctively into the personality of the unhappy Fiora – and before she knew where she was she was on the stage and the drama was unfolding.

Fiora's music is quite exacting, technically speaking, but almost more important is the projection of the drama and the subtle shift from mood to mood. It was a task peculiarly suited to Joanna's talents and, once she had conquered her initial nervousness, she found herself almost exulting in the challenge.

At the end of the first act the applause was at least as hearty as it had been on the first night. And the bass – the only complete professional in the cast – said to Joanna, 'You're better than the girl last night, good though her voice is.'

In the interval her mother came to the dressing-room, sparkling with reflected glory.

'You're splendid, darling,' she declared. 'Everyone is saying so. Elliot Cheam – nice fellow – introduced me to his uncle, and the old gentleman said you reminded him of the best Fiora he ever heard. Even that silly Oscar Warrender applauded, I noticed.'

'Mother, he is NOT silly. He only happens to be the finest conductor in the country – possibly in the world – if you must know. And the mere fact that he's here is the sort of compliment most singers would give their eye teeth for.'

'Not eye teeth, dear. They're too noticeable. Back teeth perhaps,' conceded her mother goodhumouredly. 'Anyway, don't get cross and temperamental, even if you are singing just like a prima donna. Keep on as well as you're doing now, and you can't fail. – Oh, who sent those lovely roses?'

'Elliot Cheam. But go back now, darling. I have to think myself into the second act. It's the real test.'

Her mother went immediately. And Joanna sat there at her dressing-table, put her head in her hands and thought of the guilt and the innocence and the tragedy of Fiora.

Fortunately, the bass was an excellent actor as well as singer, with something of the terrifying power needed for the old blind king. He was pleased to find that, in a mere student, he had a Fiora who could play up to him. And the tremendous scene of mounting terror and horror, culminating in the murder of the guilty girl, was played with such conviction by them both that, as he slowly groped his way from the stage, carrying her sagging body, the silence in the theatre was absolute. Indeed, for half a minute after the last chords had sounded the almost stunned silence continued, and then was succeeded by the kind of applause rarely heard at a students' performance.

In the opinion of Mrs. Ransome the third act could be nothing but an anticlimax, since all her girl had to do was to lie there 'looking very dead' as her mother put it. But the rest of the audience seemed to appreciate it, and the performance ended in a general atmosphere of congratulation and good feeling.

Oscar Warrender exchanged a few gracious words with the Principal of the College, several students in the audience asked Anthea for her autograph, and two very bold ones asked for his. But when the Principal went on to introduce Mrs. Ransome as the mother of the gifted heroine, the famous conductor acknowledged the introduction with almost the minimum degree of politeness which the occasion warranted.

Mrs. Ransome, however, was not going to leave it at that. In her view, her daughter had been done less than justice on a previous occasion, and with this very much in mind, she said boldly,

'And what did you think of her tonight, Sir Oscar?'

'She is very gifted,' replied Warrender, without specifying in what way, and then he turned away, extricated Anthea from a buzzing group of admirers, and bore her off without more ado.

Slightly deflated, though she was not quite sure why, Mrs. Ransome went backstage to Joanna's dressing-room, where she found Mr. Wilmore displaying what she considered to be a much more intelligent reaction than that of Sir Oscar. He was frankly delighted and moved by Joanna's performance, and did not hesitate to say so.

'I couldn't have done it without all the help you gave me,' Joanna said sincerely.

'My dear child, it is your own talent and hard work that are responsible,' he replied. 'I hope if there are other occasions when my collection might be of use to you, you will let me know. Even without that, please come and see me sometimes when you visit your aunt.'

Joanna said most willingly that indeed she would. And then Elliot came in, with apologies for the fact that he had been detained by friends he had not seen for some time. He added very real congratulations to those of his uncle.

'I had no idea you were so good,' he said frankly. 'I don't know why Warrender said it was not an operatic voice. I should have thought it was, and I wish you lots of luck in what ought to be a good career.'

'Sir Oscar was there, wasn't he?' Joanna tried to make that sound calm and not too eager.

'Yes. He and Anthea were mobbed by some of the students just as they were leaving.'

'They've left already, then?' She tried not to let that sound disappointed. 'Did he say anything to you about the performance?'

'No.' She thought Elliot was sorry that he had to say that. And he added, a trifle too quickly, 'He almost never goes backstage to see anyone, you know.'

'Oh, no! I didn't expect that,' said Joanna, who naturally had hoped against hope that the famous conductor would sweep in and tell her she was magnificent.

'He said you were very gifted,' her mother put in.

'*Did* he, Mother?' Joanna turned eagerly to her. 'Do you mean he volunteered the opinion – just like that?'

'No. I don't think he's generous enough to *volunteer* praise,' replied Mrs. Ransome censoriously. 'I asked him his opinion outright. I thought he deserved that.'

'Oh—' the air of eagerness faded – 'I see. Well, that's not quite the same thing, is it?'

Then she turned to the mirror and began to remove her make-up. And at this hint Elliot and his uncle took their leave. One or two other people drifted in and out, all with nothing but praise for Joanna's performance, and she managed somehow to look and sound elated and happy.

She *was* elated and happy, of course. She knew she had done her very best, and she had been a resounding success. – But Oscar Warrender had left the theatre without a word to her and, try as she would, she could not help feeling that somehow, somewhere she had failed.

Joanna made every effort to hide from her mother the fact that the evening had in some way disappointed her. She said she was tired, that she was feeling the reaction after all the work and strain, and that was why she could not eat much supper and why she really just wanted to go to bed.

'Of course, my dear – of course!' Her mother seemed to regard this as the perfectly understandable behaviour of a nearly fledged prima donna. Indeed, she would possibly have been disappointed if Joanna had shown her usual good appetite and cheerful disposition.

'Being murdered – even on the stage – must take it out of one,' was her original explanation. 'You go to bed, darling, and I'll bring you something nice on a tray. Just some soup, perhaps, and a little bit of cold chicken. And then you shall have a good night's rest, and when you wake up you'll have forgotten all about it.'

Presumably she meant all about being murdered. Anyway, Joanna accepted her suggestion thankfully, had her light supper in bed and then, to her subsequent surprise, fell straight asleep and slept dreamlessly until she woke to find her mother shaking her gently and saying,

'I'm so sorry, Joanna dear, but could you wake up and take a phone call? He's very insistent?'

'Who is?' muttered Joanna. 'And what is the time?'

'It's ten o'clock. And I don't know who it is on the phone. Someone very *sure* of himself. If it didn't seem so improbable, I'd say it was that Oscar Warrender, but—'

'*Mother!*' Joanna was instantly wide awake and out of bed, groping for her dressing-gown which she flung around her as she ran downstairs.

'Hello,' she said breathlessly into the phone. 'It's me – Joanna Ransome, I mean. Who is that, please?'

'Oscar Warrender. I apologize if I have roused you too early, but I have to go out—'

'It's quite all right. I just happened to sleep a little late after the performance. But – can I do anything for you?'

She thought immediately that the words sounded idiotic from a struggling student to a famous man, and he seemed to find it rather funny too. At any rate, there was a hint of amusement in that cool, incisive voice as he replied,

'Yes, you can. You can come along and see me this afternoon at three o'clock. Do you know the address? Killigrew Mansions, St. James's. The porter will bring you up.'

'Yes, I'll be there,' Joanna promised, quite breathless again, but this time not with running. 'And, Sir Oscar—'

'I have no time to discuss anything else at the moment,' he cut in, pleasantly but firmly. 'But I would advise you not to talk about this appointment with anyone else at present.'

'Very well,' Joanna said meekly and as she heard the receiver replaced at the other end, she wondered if even her mother were to be included in this injunction.

Of course, *any* appointment which Oscar Warrender might make with a singer must carry with it a sort of news value, and he was obviously warning her against talking too confidently or too soon about — what?

There was nothing in his words or tone to give her the slightest clue. But she felt she must obey him to the letter. And so, when she rejoined her mother, she simply said, 'It was Sir Oscar. He — and his wife—' she added in a moment of inspiration, 'want me to go to tea there this afternoon. Perhaps it's their way of making up for not coming round to see me after the performance last night.'

Probably no one but Mrs. Ransome would have regarded this as likely behaviour on the part of a famous conductor and his equally famous wife. But she had been reading the uniformly good Press notices and saw no reason why *any*one should be less than eager to meet her wonderful daughter and make much of her.

With difficulty Joanna concealed her own overwhelming excitement and curiosity about the afternoon's appointment. And in this she was helped by the many telephone calls of congratulation and the happy perusal of her Press notices.

Later she did a little practising, in case Sir Oscar should, for some reason, want to hear her sing again. Then, having dithered for at least ten minutes over what she should wear, she chose what she hoped was a suitable compromise between the elegance demanded by what might be a distinguished social call and the plain restraint of something which would make her look like a very serious student.

The moment she was shown into the big studio in the Warrenders' handsome apartment she knew it mattered not at all what she wore, and she wondered momentarily why she had ever supposed it should. The whole place was suggestive of dedicated work, and those who came or went merely added to or detracted from the purpose of the man who greeted her.

'Sit down, Miss Joanna.' He conceded that degree of informality to the occasion, but gave the impression of having no time to waste on social preliminaries. 'Tell me – was last night the first time you had been on stage?'

'No, not quite.' Joanna explained briefly about her modest experience in the touring company and her few other college performances.

'I see. Who has been responsible for your actual stage training? As distinct from whatever is included in your college curriculum, I mean.'

'Why, no one.' She looked slightly puzzled. 'I've had no extra tuition, if that's what you mean.'

'That is what I mean,' he told her. 'Have you ever studied mime? apart from whatever might be taken along with general stage technique?'

'No,' Joanna shook her head.

'Interesting,' he observed. 'Do you sight-read well?'

'M-moderately well.' She glanced nervously in the direction of the piano.

'There's no need to be frightened,' he told her, assessing her mood at once. 'Come over here and see if you can sight-read this for me.'

She went with him to the piano and accepted the manuscript score which he put into her hands, with the injunction to study it for a few minutes.

This she did, wishing all the time that she could keep the pages from trembling quite so obviously. Then, after a few minutes, she began to be attracted by what she was examining. The words were in English and obviously formed the end of some work, and as she hummed the main air to herself she was aware that there was a compelling and most appealing simplicity about it.

'I've never come across this before.' She looked up and across at the conductor, who was now seated at the piano.

'No. No one has ever sung it before,' he replied coolly, and his words sent a current of extraordinary excitement through her.

'I think I could read it all right. Shall I stand behind you and read over your shoulder?'

'No. I know the work by heart – at least, that part of it. Keep the manuscript with you. And tell me what you have gathered from the words.'

'It's – it's a simple but impassioned plea for love – someone's love, isn't it? With a sort of implication of tremendous sacrifice. And at the high point of the aria – she dies.'

'Correct. Sing it for me.'

Instinctively, she remembered his previous order to stand where he could see her, so she came and stood in the curve of the grand piano and turned to face him. To her mortification, she made a false start, but he was unexpectedly patient, showed her where she had made an unnecessary difficulty for herself, and gave her plenty of time to begin again.

The second time she managed better, and after the first page she found herself profoundly moved and intrigued by the beauty of the music and the way it merged with the words in a complete synthesis of the two modes of expression.

She sang it through to the end, and exclaimed, 'It's quite lovely, isn't it?'

'I think so. Try it again. And now that you are a

little more familiar with it, give me some light and shade in the music and more expression in your face.'

She did exactly as he bade her. And at the end he said 'Yes.' That was all. But the one word expressed a sort of pleased confirmation of something he had already thought.

He took the manuscript from her and, still holding it in his hand, led her back to the other end of the room, where they had first sat and talked. For a moment there was silence, while Joanna's heart thumped with excitement and the curious conviction that some tremendous step was about to be taken. The conductor, on his side, seemed to be choosing his words with some care.

'Have you ever heard of a man called Bernard Fulroyd?' he asked, and Joanna obediently searched back in her memory.

'The name is familiar.' She hesitated. 'Didn't he compose a lovely song cycle that was given at some music festival last year?'

'Yes, that's right. His daughter sang the solo part — very beautifully, I might say. The work caused something of a sensation and is already being included in concerts here and abroad. He is an organist in a small town, quite an elderly man, and this was the first of his works to be performed in public, except for some fairly unimportant items for choir and organ performed in the local church.'

He paused for a moment and Joanna leaned forward and asked eagerly, 'And is this work by him too?'

'Yes. It's one of several operas he has composed. All of them contain at least a large proportion of good, often exceptionally beautiful, music. But each one has some nearly insurmountable practical difficulty about it which almost precludes performance. He is a completely unworldly type. Possibly that is why his music has this extraordinary basic simplicity and beauty. He writes what he feels he must write without the smallest idea of the technical difficulties involved in bringing the work to production.'

'But this is a most lovely and accessible air,' protested Joanna, 'and surely – I should have thought – a most fitting end to an opera.'

'Agreed,' said Warrender dryly. 'But that is the only – and I mean literally the only – music given to the heroine. Which kills it stone dead, of course, so far as most leading singers are concerned. The prima donna who is willing to wait until the end of the last act before she opens her mouth does not, in my experience, exist.'

'Oh – I see,' said Joanna doubtfully.

'And yet, dramatically, the part demands the highest degree of acting ability. An exceptionally fine actress could play the whole role – up to the last quarter of an hour. But for that last quarter of an hour she must be able to sing so well that there is no sense of anticlimax.'

'Yes – I see,' said Joanna again, and the sense of excitement which had been growing within her suddenly engulfed her like a wave. She gasped slightly, passed the tip of her tongue over suddenly dry lips and asked, 'What exactly is the story of the opera? I mean – what is actually involved?'

'Briefly, it is the age-old story which appears in one form or another in various works of art. In Hans Andersen's "Little Mermaid", for instance, and in the Czech opera "Russalka". The heroine is a half fairy creature who loves, and is loved by, a prince of earth. Her choice has offended the deities of her fairy world, who deprive her of her power of speech if she insists on going with him. Or rather, she is warned that if she speaks she will die. She accepts the terms – and the risk – and goes with him.'

'Which is why the poor thing can't sing a note for two and a half acts!' exclaimed Joanna.

'Exactly. You see how little that would appeal to almost any distinguished soprano one could name,' Warrender said dryly. 'My wife declares it would be almost worth it for the impact one would make with that one last superb scene. But she says – and I think correctly – that though she is a good actress, she has not the tremendous range of facial expression nor the power to convey with movement – or the lack of it – exactly what is required.'

'And are you—' Joanna's voice shook with excitement – 'are you suggesting that I *have* that power?'

'I think,' Warrender said slowly, 'you have almost exactly the rare combination of talents required. You have one of the most innocent and yet expressive faces I have seen in an adult. You have the quality of portraying fear and longing and innocent simplicity in the way you walk and stand and move. You even convey an extraordinary amount when you are still, which is perhaps the rarest gift of all. The voice is good enough for that one final outburst; particularly if I have the handling of you,' he added, and a slight note of ruthlessness entered his voice at those words.

'Are you,' said Joanna in a very small voice, 'offering me the part?'

'I'm suggesting that you study it intensively. You'll need some very strict and very expensive dramatic training, but I know exactly to whom to send you. It may all come to nothing in the end. I must, in all fairness, tell you that. Because, of course, one can fully prepare a work and still be a long way from putting it before the public. One has to start somewhere, however, and one has to take calculated risks if one is to achieve anything. Your risk would be that you would be diverted from your more conventional training into something absolutely specialized. If, in spite of everything, the work never saw the light of day, you might, by your own reckoning, consider that you had wasted your time, your talents and a good deal of money.'

'But—' again she passed her tongue over her dry lips — 'suppose it succeeded, in the way you visualize?'

'Then in that case, my dear, I have little doubt that you would find yourself famous overnight,' said Oscar Warrender coolly.

CHAPTER SIX

JOANNA was not quite sure how long she sat there, digesting the extraordinary information Oscar Warrender had given her. Not that she had any doubt about acceptance or refusal. One did not, she supposed, *refuse* a project which the great Warrender thought might bring one fame. It was just that she had to allow the stunning truth to permeate her whole being.

He made no attempt to hurry her. Instead, he sat opposite her, apparently re-examining the score with close attention, and not until she said, hesitatingly, 'Sir Oscar—' did he look up.

'Yes?' He smiled encouragingly. 'Does the prospect interest you?'

'Interest me? It stuns me,' Joanna said frankly. 'I find it very difficult to believe myself capable of fulfilling such a task. It's far, far beyond my wildest ambitions.'

'That is because up to now you have thought only in terms of what you can do rather well,' he told her. 'And never in terms of something you might be able to do uniquely well.'

'I don't expect you to go on reassuring me.' Joanna spoke almost apologetically. 'But I suppose it's always difficult to imagine one might be supremely gifted in some form or another.'

'On the contrary,' replied the conductor dryly, 'it is astonishing the ease with which some people imagine themselves to be supremely gifted, on practically no evidence at all. You are unusually modest – a pleasing trait, of course, but not an attitude to be pursued to the point of self-denigration. I am not suggesting for one moment that you are at this present time ready to shake the world with your performance of this role or any other. I am merely saying that you possess unusual gifts which, developed to their highest point, might make a very interesting artist of you. Particularly so in this difficult role, which could well fail in the hands of much greater singers than you will ever be.'

'You are *sure* about this?' she said timidly.

'No, my dear. Only fools are absolutely sure about another human being in advance,' he replied with a smile. 'But, speaking from not inconsiderable experience, I think the strong probability is there, provided you will work as directed, develop as expected and, in some way, attract that minimum degree of sheer luck which is essential to almost every worthwhile undertaking. Does that make it easier – or more difficult – to make up your mind?'

'Oh, I have no difficulty in making up my mind,' she assured him. 'It's the kind of millionth chance which no one would have the effrontery even to hope for in ordinary circumstances. If the practical details can be worked out to your satisfaction, of course I accept. Sir Oscar, of *course* I do!'

'Good,' he said, and she noticed a slight streak of colour in his cheeks and, incredulously, she realized that she had in some way excited him by her decision.

'You said at one point,' she reminded him, 'that some very expensive training would be involved. What exactly do you mean by "expensive"?'

He laughed slightly at that.

'It is rather a relative term,' he agreed. 'Ideally – in fact, I think essentially – you would have to go to Tamara Volnikov. Do you know who I mean?'

'She was a dancer a long time ago, wasn't she?'

'I suppose it was a long time ago by your reckoning,' he agreed with an amused little grimace. 'At any rate, it was in my youth that I saw her. She was already near the end of her career then. But she could express more with one gesture or glance than most stage people can convey in a whole scene. She is quite an old woman now. A greedy old woman, if I am frank,' he added impersonally. 'She occasionally takes a pupil, but only if she is interested, and her fees are shamelessly high. But then if you are unique it is fair that you should name your price. I don't know exactly what she charges. We should have to find out – always provided she thought you worth her notice, of course.'

'I think I ought to say at this point that – that my mother and I are not specially well off,' Joanna said a little agitated. 'But I'm sure she would be willing for us to sacrifice a good deal in order for me to get the essential training.'

'Well, that is a proper outlook, in my view. But I was also going to say that last night I had a few words with Justin Wilmore, who is also convinced that you are unusually gifted—'

'But only because I remind him of Emilia Trangoni,' cried Joanna distressedly.

'No, not only that,' Warrender corrected her, 'though there is that element, I admit. The fact is that the special quality you possess stirs the roots of memory. *Everyone's* memory. It is something both basic and universal and, properly developed, channelled and trained, it will take you a long way. But – and please remember this above anything else I have said – without the work necessary to perfect this, you will be no more than an occasionally admired performer who wonders why she never gets any further. The same is true of every real artist, believe me.'

'I do believe you,' Joanna said humbly. 'And I'll work.'

'Very well. What I was going to say about Justin Wilmore is that he also believes you worthy of a chance and, in frank, practical fact, is willing to supply whatever money is necessary for your specialized training, if your own resources do not run to this.'

'He's too good,' exclaimed Joanna anxiously. 'I don't think I could accept that from him. You see—'

'Don't bore me with how you can or cannot avail yourself of opportunities offered,' Warrender cut in impatiently. 'That is between you, your bank manager and Justin Wilmore. I shall merely tell you the artistic essentials, and you must decide what you can do unaided and where you may require help. This is only the beginning. Later it will be my business to decide how much backing is required, by me or anyone else, actually to put on the work. Let us take one step at a time. And the first step is for you to familiarize yourself with this work in every detail, and then I'll take you to Volnikov.'

'Thank you very, very much.' Joanna drew a long sigh of mingled rapture and worry. For, in her view, the very first step was to find out how far she and her mother could finance her training for this incredible undertaking.

'Again let me emphasize that the less you say about this to *anyone* at this stage, the better. Nothing is easier to start than some rumour that an operatic or theatrical sensation is in the offing. If the whole thing goes off at half-cock it can be an embarrassment and a disaster, and I do not care to be associated with either,' he added disdainfully.

Joanna wanted to say that she would not like the experience either. But she guessed that her feelings in the matter were of little importance to the great man until she had proved herself much further than she had been able to do so far. He regarded her as good raw material. She doubted if, even now, he regarded her as much else. But apparently she was the type of raw material necessary to his enterprise, and as such she had a certain value for him.

'May I tell my mother most of the truth?' she asked after a moment. 'Her agreement will be an essential part of my involvement.'

'You mean she holds the purse-strings?'

'I mean,' said Joanna, disliking the expression, 'that she's a widow and, apart from small fees from time to time, I'm dependent on her. In other words, I can't make free with her money unless I give good reasons for whatever I suggest.'

'All right,' he said, rather reluctantly. 'But impress upon her that there must be no exulting beforehand.'

'I will,' promised Joanna, uncomfortably aware that Warrender had probably summed up her mother pretty accurately in the space of time it had taken to exchange a couple of sentences.

Then he showed her out. And Joanna walked most of the way home, past newspaper placards bearing threats of war in some distant country, the failure of a big investment company nearer home, and a prophecy of the hardest winter for fifty years. None of these made the slightest impression upon her. All she knew was that Oscar Warrender had made an unbelievably exciting proposition to her, and that this was the turning point of her life.

When she reached home she was tired with walking and still dazed by the incredible thing that had happened to her. But even so, as she came into the sitting-room she was immediately struck by the extraordinary stillness of her mother, who was sitting by the fire, her hands slack in her lap, her gaze oddly unfocused, like someone who had experienced a great shock.

'Mother!' Forgetting her own affairs, Joanna ran forward in dismay. 'What is it? What has happened?'

'Where have you been?' Her mother's glance came round to her, but not with complete attention.

'I've been to see Oscar Warrender. Don't you remember he—?'

'Oh, yes. You were going to tea with them, weren't you? They didn't keep you long—' Her glance shifted absently to the clock.

In retrospect it seemed to Joanna that she had passed a lifetime of experience since she had left home, but she brushed that aside and, putting her hand insistently on her mother's shoulder, she repeated, 'What's happened? You've had some kind of shock, haven't you?'

'Yes. Naturally it's a shock.'

'But *what* is?' cried Joanna urgently.

'Haven't you seen the newspaper placards?'

'No,' Joanna said. For, in all accuracy, she had not seen them. She had merely walked past them without a thought.

'The Home and Overseas Insurance Company have gone broke – taking half our income with them. Mr.

Witherspoon rang up to tell me, and he said it's in all the evening papers and on the radio. He also said – which I thought was mean of him – that he was always against my investing with them, because the rate of interest was suspiciously high.'

'And *was* he always against it?' asked Joanna, because she felt she had to ask something.

'Yes, of course. But then lawyers are always over-cautious, aren't they?' replied her mother plaintively.

Joanna resisted the obvious reply that in this case Mr. Witherspoon's caution seemed to have been justified, for her mother looked so forlorn and bewildered that any form of 'I told you so' seemed like cruelty to children. Instead, she addressed herself to offering some form of comfort and reassurance.

'Don't worry too much, darling,' she urged. 'We'll manage – we always have. And often these things aren't so bad as everyone thinks at first. Anyway, the house is ours—'

'There's a mortgage on it.'

'Is – is there?' Joanna suddenly dared not ask how much, and she wondered for the first time why she had taken what seemed now to be criminally little interest in the way her mother managed their financial affairs. But then, strictly speaking, they had been her mother's financial affairs, and sometimes she had been oddly secretive about them.

Well, it was no good thinking about that now. And as Mrs. Ransome said rather pathetically at this moment that she thought she could do with a cup of tea, Joanna went into the kitchen to put on the kettle. As she stood there waiting for it to boil, her thoughts veered from one extreme of improbability to another.

On the one hand was the extraordinary golden vista which Oscar Warrender had opened before her, and on the other something like ruin, financially speaking. Neither seemed quite real at this moment.

Over tea Joanna strove to find some other words of comfort.

'It's really just a question of bridging the gap, isn't it?' she said cheerfully. 'It won't be all that long before I am earning money, Mother. Perhaps quite big money,' she added encouragingly.

'What makes you say that?' Her mother's face brightened a little. 'Did Oscar Warrender offer you a part or something?'

'N-not exactly. But he had some very interesting things to say about my future development. It would mean quite a lot of specialized training,' she admitted. But as this did not seem to be the moment to talk about Madame Volnikov and her expensive lessons, she added hastily, 'He had ideas about how that could be managed. And he seemed to think that, given luck—'

'Our luck doesn't seem to be in at the moment,' interrupted Mrs. Ransome with a sad little laugh.

'Then it's time for it to change,' asserted Joanna firmly. 'He really did seem to see a very bright future for me, Mother.'

'But how far ahead?' asked her mother, who had a talent for sometimes putting her finger right on the first awkward essential.

'I'm not – quite sure,' Joanna confessed. And, for the first time, a dreadful chill gripped her, and she wondered if perhaps, after all, she were fated never to reach that shining goal which Oscar Warrender had allowed her to glimpse for a moment.

If they were really going to have to look twice at

every penny in future, what was the use of thinking in terms of expensive extra training? The money for that would have to come from *somewhere*.

And then she recalled what Warrender had said about generous Mr. Wilmore. Although her first reaction was to wince away from any thought of appealing to him, again and again during the rather sad evening which succeeded the madly exciting afternoon, her mind returned to him. Was he not the best – possibly the only – source for the help she would need to fulfil the extraordinary destiny which still seemed to beckon her, though not quite so clearly as it had seemed to do in Warrender's studio?

The next few days were confused and frightening. No one seemed to know quite what might be the final outcome of the crash which had taken place, though Mr. Witherspoon kept them as well informed as he could and was not unencouraging about the possibility of something being saved from the wreck.

Joanna, meanwhile, kept her extravagant hopes to herself. She dared not make plans, and still less could she discuss such plans with her mother, who was naturally in no mood to discuss anything which would involve any immediate financial outlay.

Then, very much earlier than she had expected such a development, Warrender telephoned to her again and informed her that he wished to take her to see Madame Volnikov that afternoon. Would she please be ready to be picked up by car at two-thirty?

'But I haven't learned anything of the part yet!' she exclaimed in dismay.

'Naturally not, since I have not given you a copy of the work yet,' replied Warrender. 'But Madame Volnikov wants to see you and test you in her own way before she will say whether or not she will take you on.'

Joanna thought for a moment of telling him about the new and alarming complication. But why should he be interested? In any case, if the old dancer decided against taking her as a pupil the question of the expensive lessons would not even arise.

So she promised to be ready. And when Warrender's car drew up outside, she ran out quickly, determined neither to keep him waiting nor to give her mother any chance to ask awkward questions. She had already explained casually that she had to go to an extra lesson and that someone would be picking her up from home. That the someone was driving a Bentley might, in ordinary circumstances, have intrigued her mother. But in her present mood she did not even glance out of the window.

Joanna slipped into the seat beside the conductor and asked shyly if they had far to go.

'Oh, no. Less than twenty minutes' drive.'

'Do you know her quite well, Sir Oscar?' Somehow she felt a little less in awe of him when he was not immediately concerned with observing her work.

'Not socially. Only as artists of a certain calibre usually know and assess each other,' he said with a slight smile. And then they were silent until they reached the house where the old dancer lived.

It was in one of the northern suburbs which had once been very fashionable but now looked slightly dilapidated. Here and there were still signs of faded elegance, and the house before which they stopped was quite imposing. It stood back from the quiet avenue, and trees not only shaded it but almost engulfed it, giving it a secret and slightly sad air.

They were admitted by an elderly manservant who looked incredibly like someone out of the only Chekhov play Joanna had ever seen, and were shown into a splendid room furnished in a manner that would not have disgraced a museum of fine arts.

Joanna wondered if even Oscar Warrender felt slightly intimidated. But if so he concealed the fact, crossing the room to examine a particularly fine picture with genuine interest. Then the door opened again and their hostess came in.

Joanna had somehow expected a little old lady. What she saw was a completely ageless woman of medium height, who moved with such flowing grace that she hardly seemed to walk. Afterwards Joanna could not remember at all what she wore. She only knew that her figure, her movements, her clothes were all in one harmonious whole which was grace personified.

Her face was pure oval, entirely innocent of make-up, with the high, flat cheekbones of the almost oriental Slav, and long, dark eyes of burning intelligence and beauty.

She greeted Warrender rather as the Queen of Sheba might have greeted Solomon, according him almost royal status but reserving the right to regard herself as just one degree more royal, as it were.

'And this is the little girl you spoke of?' She surveyed Joanna kindly, but somewhat as she might have looked at a child on its first day in the kindergarten. 'Walk the length of the room, dear.'

The form of address had nothing affectionate about it. It carried, in fact, a note of absolute command, so that Joanna obeyed her instantly. But as she walked the length of the room she felt as though she had clogs on her feet, and could only pray that she would not slip or stumble. Then she turned and came back, while the Russian – and indeed Warrender too – watched her intently.

'Hm—' said Madame Volnikov. 'What were you expressing then?'

'*Expressing?*' Joanna considered that. 'Awkwardness, I should think, and a nervous hope that I wouldn't stumble. I felt a bit like a camel,' she admitted.

'You looked rather like one, dear,' Madame Volnikov said with some asperity. 'Now forget about me – and even the handsome Sir Oscar – for the moment. You are a young girl, expecting to meet the man you love. You are carrying a basket – here you are—' Incredibly she produced a basket as a conjuror might and put it into Joanna's hand – 'you go quickly towards him, and suddenly realize it is not he, after all, but the person in the world you most fear. – Go on.'

'Walking *away* from you, do you mean?'

'Yes.'

'But you can't see my face!'

'I don't want to see your face. I want to see your back.'

'Very well.' Joanna stood quite still for half a minute, thinking herself into the suggested scene. She wondered where the catch was. She wondered what she could possibly do to make the whole thing stunningly effective. And she could think of nothing – absolutely nothing. Except just what she herself would do if presented with the situation.

It was all useless, of course. She knew it was. But she must at least attempt to do what she had been told to do, and then apologize for having none of what this extraordinary woman seemed to expect of her.

She half ran up the long room, lightly swinging her basket in a carefree way. Then, in imagination, she actually *saw* the person she was to be afraid of and stopped, instinctively tensing every muscle before letting her arm drop to her side in a futile attempt to repeat that careless swinging of the basket.

'I'll take her,' said Madame Volnikov.

'Ah—!' said Warrender on a note of undoubted satisfaction.

'But why?' asked Joanna, turning and coming slowly back to where the other two were standing. 'I mean – why do you think, on such small evidence, that I'm worth your attention?'

The older woman smiled.

'Because, with the most economical means possible, you both touched and terrified me within the space of two minutes.'

'But I didn't do anything special.' Joanna looked puzzled.

'No. Real artists don't *do*. They *are*. Your actions and reactions are purely instinctive and right. You have a great deal to learn, *chérie*. But you have come to the right person to teach you.' There was no false modesty about that. 'It will cost you a lot of money, but it will be worth every penny. Now we will have tea.'

So the most magnificent samovar was brought in, and Madame Volnikov dispensed tea in cups so fragile and beautiful that Joanna was frightened every time she touched hers. She left most of the conversation to Warrender, and it was he who explained about the interesting opera in which he hoped Joanna would appear.

'Nothing but movement and facial expression until

the very end?' Madame Volnikov smiled. 'A big undertaking, but tremendously challenging. Does the child actually sing well also?'

'Very reasonably well.' Warrender, like the Russian, spoke as though Joanna were not present. 'Not a great voice, but an appealing voice, well used. Capable of a fine climax, but not capable of sustained power and intensity throughout a whole evening. The opera might have been written for her. Provided she does the work.'

'Oh, yes. Provided she works.' Madame Volnikov looked searchingly at Joanna then. 'Are you a dedicated worker, child?'

'I should like to believe so.' Joanna smiled at her. 'And I think you, Madame, would inspire anyone.'

'Not anyone. Most people are incapable of inspiration,' was the cold reply. 'Who is financing her, Warrender?'

Joanna, who had never thought to hear Sir Oscar addressed in this summary way, glanced quickly at him.

'Miss Joanna and her mother hope to find some of the backing, and I know of a musical patron who may be expected to do the rest.'

'A wealthy musical patron, I hope,' said Madame Volnikov with great frankness.

'Moderately so,' replied Warrender smoothly. 'Do you wish to discuss that now?'

'No. I will write. It is better to have these things in writing.' An expression of quite extraordinary cupidity passed over that arresting face. Then she turned once more to Joanna and said, 'Little one, do you know how to cry real tears, to order?'

'I – don't think so.'

'I will teach you.' The old woman smiled at her, the most beautiful smile Joanna had ever seen. 'You will need tears for this part. We are going to enjoy ourselves, you and I. When can you start?'

Joanna did some rapid and, to tell the truth desperate, calculations. She must familiarize herself with the part and, even more important, she must somehow go to see Mr. Wilmore and enlist his help. For how else was she to take this amazing – this unprecedented – chance?

'In about two weeks' time,' she said with decision.

'It is not a desperate matter,' the dancer told her, with a curious glance.

'No, I know,' said Joanna quickly.

'And yet desperation was there in your face for a moment. *Everything* is there in her face,' observed Madame Volnikov to Warrender, 'for those who have eyes to see. And when she has been trained – by me – she will be able to project that for even the fools to see.'

Then she got up, with the air of a queen dismissing her court. And Joanna and Warrender took their leave.

'Do you think,' asked Joanna when they were back once more in the car, 'that she was *really* able to assess me on that little scene?'

'Oh, yes. I could even, to a certain extent, see myself what she meant. But remember,' he went on sternly, 'all this is only the *promise* of what might be. It is usually a mistake to give compliments and too much praise at such an early stage. In your case these things had to be said, otherwise you would see no reason to change into such a specialized course. But none of it – and I mean *none* of it – will be of the slightest use unless

130

you do the necessary work.'

'I do know that! I truly do – and I will work,' Joanna promised. 'And then,' she added timidly, 'there's the problem of the money to pay for the lessons. She made it sound as though they were going to cost the earth, didn't she?'

'She did indeed! And she looked it too. One wishes a really fine artist could have captured that amazing face when she spoke of the money, and then when she smiled.'

'It was a beautiful smile,' Joanna exclaimed in all honesty.

'Ravishing,' he agreed. 'But not a smile to knock anything off the bill, I imagine.'

Joanna laughed reluctantly. But then she spoke with some decision.

'Sir Oscar, I realize that I haven't really come to grips with the situation until now. My mother has singularly little capital behind her, and I can't just go scrounging to Mr. Wilmore. I must get a job – and as quickly as possible.'

'What sort of a job?' asked the conductor disagreeably.

'*Any* job that will bring in some money. I'm not afraid of hard work, and although I'm not specially well qualified for anything like office work, I'd be prepared to be a waitress, a shop assistant – I don't mind what, so long as I could pay for my lessons with that extraordinary woman.'

'Quite impossible,' said Warrender briefly.

'What do you mean – quite impossible?' She turned in her seat and looked at him.

'I don't think you understand even now that, during the next few months, you are going to have to work and study as you have never done before in your life. You're not going to be just a conscientious little student, doing your daily stint. You are going to be a dedicated slave to one single idea. And when Volnikov and I have finished with you, you won't have any energy left for anything but to fall into bed and sleep long enough to gather strength for the next test.'

'O-Oh—' Joanna was not so dismayed by the prospect as disappointed that her solution to the money problem had been thus brushed aside. 'Do you *really* think,' she said slowly at last, 'that I can apply to Mr. Wilmore?'

'I thought that was already agreed,' replied Warrender with a touch of impatience. 'Will you write to him?'

She hesitated for a moment, hoping that perhaps he would add, 'Or shall I?' But he said no such thing, presumably thinking that now she must act for herself.

'No. I shall go and see him,' Joanna stated. 'If one is asking for a favour one should face the person concerned.'

'Possibly you're right.' The conductor looked amused. Then he relented sufficiently to say, 'You may tell Wilmore that I suggested you should approach him.' Then, as they arrived outside Joanna's house, he reached into a compartment at the front of the car, produced a photostat copy of the score and handed it to her.

'Study it well,' he advised her. 'And good luck.'

She thanked him for the score, and then even more fervently for taking her to see Madame Volnikov, and ran into the house, full of the wildest excitement and the most agitating anxieties. Fortunately, her mother showed remarkably little curiosity in her goings and comings these days and no questions were asked. But she did look up sharply when Joanna said, some time during the evening,

'You know, I think I shall go down and see Aunt Georgina this week-end. She hasn't been up for some while, and I haven't been to her since that first time I went to Wilmore Grange.'

'Why do you want to see her?' objected Mrs. Ransome. 'Not to tell her about the mess we're in? She'll just be censorious and want to tell me what I ought to have done, now it's too late to do it.'

'I wasn't thinking of telling her much.'

'Why tell her anything?' Mrs. Ransome sounded fretful. 'And why go just now, anyway?'

'Because I should like to look in on Mr. Wilmore at the same time,' Joanna explained as casually as she could. 'He showed such kind interest in my Fiora that I think I should keep in touch with him, don't you?'

'I suppose – yes,' her mother agreed doubtfully. 'It all seems such a long time ago, that lovely, happy evening, doesn't it? I don't seem able to think about anything nowadays but the trouble we're in.'

'Mother dear, try to think about something else for a change! We aren't absolutely looking for the next penny, are we, now? And do believe me when I say I really think my career is going to blossom quite soon. Several people have spoken to me about that Fiora performance and – further possibilities. It's just a case of the darkest hour before dawn and all that sort of thing.'

'You think so?' For the first time Joanna saw her mother give something like her old childlike smile. 'Wouldn't it be *wonderful* if all our worries could be

133

over and we be happy again?'

A good deal touched, Joanna said that indeed it would. Then she telephoned to Aunt Georgina and arranged to go down to see her the following Saturday.

'By the way, didn't your mother have some money in that wretched Home and Overseas Insurance Company?' inquired her aunt.

'Y-yes, a bit, I think,' replied Joanna cautiously.

'So did I, unfortunately,' was the unexpected reply. 'Well, I suppose we're all fools at some time in our lives. I shall be glad to see you, Joanna. And you had better go along and call on Mr. Wilmore while you're here. I met him in the village the other day and he spoke about you and said he hoped to see you soon. Apparently he was very much impressed with that performance of yours.'

'Oh, Aunt Georgina, I'm so glad!' Joanna's spirits bounded up at this news. For it seemed much less shameful to go to see Mr. Wilmore in answer to a repeated invitation of his than just to appear on his doorstep with a request for financial aid.

'Did she say anything about the Home and Overseas crash?' Mrs. Ransome wanted to know, as soon as Joanna came away from the telephone.

'Yes, she did. She dropped some money on it herself.'

'Oh *poor* Georgina!' exclaimed Mrs. Ransome, the greatest relief irradiating her face. And, although there was not a grain of real malice in her, she cheered up from that moment and began to be a little more her usual self.

When Joanna arrived at her aunt's bungalow on the Saturday she found her looking pretty well *her* usual self too. Whatever her loss had been she seemed to be taking it philosophically, though she did volunteer the remark that no one liked to see good savings swept away.

'But then,' she added, 'I never put enough into any one thing to court disaster. I trust it was the same with Pansy?'

'Something the same,' Joanna murmured somewhat disingenuously. And then she added quickly, 'It's really rather extraordinary that you should both have been involved.'

'Not extraordinary at all,' retorted her aunt briskly, 'It was a fairly widespread concern. Quite a number of people in this part of the country dropped a packet, as the vulgar expression is. It seems there was a specially active branch in the district and it was a popular form of investment. Well, as I said, we are all fools some time in our lives. When do you propose to call on Mr. Wilmore?'

'I thought – this afternoon,' said Joanna. And her heart took an uneasy plunge as she heard herself definitely committed to an exact time for the interview she dreaded.

It was useless for her to tell herself that the original suggestion had come from Mr. Wilmore himself – in general terms to her and, apparently, in more specific to Sir Oscar. The fact was that Joanna was not among the people who can lightly ask other people for money without feeling that somehow there is an element of cadging in the exercise.

Once more her aunt drove her to the Grange and left her at the gate, and Joanna could not help remembering vividly that first time she had come, and how angry Elliot had been with her – and how suspicious.

Almost as though in some way he foresaw what she was doing now!

What on earth would he think of her present errand? she wondered as she tugged at the brass bell-pull. And at the thought of that she almost turned tail and ran. But the door was opened at that moment, and the servant smiled an undoubted welcome.

In answer to her inquiry, he said that Mr. Wilmore was in the garden, and if Miss Ransome would go through the drawing-room and across the terrace she would probably find him there.

Miss Ransome went, a little relieved in her mind at this friendly reception. And then, as she entered the drawing-room, a graceful figure uncurled itself from the sofa, and Sara Fernie stood up and said, 'Hello! What brings *you* here?'

CHAPTER SEVEN

The shock of finding Sara Fernie almost literally in her path momentarily robbed Joanna of speech. Then, with a tremendous effort, she rallied her defences.

'I came down to visit my aunt,' she explained. 'And as Mr. Wilmore had asked me to call in if I were in the district, I came along.'

'I see.' Sara's amused glance passed over her in a way that was singularly unnerving. 'You'll find him in the garden, if you want anything.'

'So I've been told.' Joanna gave her a curt little nod and went out on to the terrace. But, as she descended the few steps to the garden, Sara's last words rang unpleasantly in her ears. It was almost as though the other girl had penetrated her thoughts and knew that she did indeed want something desperately.

Joanna had not entirely recovered her composure by the time she came upon Mr. Wilmore. But the familiar kindness of his welcome, and his undoubted pleasure in seeing her, calmed her quivering nerves.

'I was just telling your aunt last week that I hoped you would come and see me if you were visiting her,' he said.

'She passed on the message. Which is why I plucked up the courage to come,' Joanna assured him.

'Did it require any effort of courage?' He raised his eyebrows in protest. 'I didn't realize I was such an ogre.'

'Oh, you're *not*!' cried Joanna. 'Only, when someone has been exceptionally kind already, one feels awful if one has to come and ask for a further favour. And – and that's what I've come to do.'

'Even that doesn't call for an effort of courage between friends,' he replied charmingly. 'What is it? My collection is entirely at your disposal for any further study. Is that it?'

'N-not this time,' she confessed. 'It's something more personal and – difficult.' And then, diffidently but with a certain degree of resolution, she told him of Oscar Warrender's belief that she had the qualities to score a great success in a work as yet unheard and unseen.

'He said – I have to tell you this in order to justify my presuming to come to you – that if I worked hard and had the right coaching I might well find myself famous overnight. But very specialized teaching would be necessary, and the ideal person to give that would be an old dancer called Tamara Volnikov—'

'I remember her very well,' Mr. Wilmore put in. 'Extraordinary creature! Unlikeable, but an undoubted genius.'

'Sir Oscar took me to her. She gave me what seemed to me a most perfunctory sort of test and then instantly agreed to take me. She said some strange and complimentary things about me which I still find hard to believe, but which Sir Oscar cautiously endorsed. And the upshot was that if – if the money can be found I shall become her pupil for some intensive months of training. Both she and Sir Oscar seem confident that I'm worthy of their efforts.'

'Then, my dear, there can be no question about it,' was the emphatic reply. 'I find it unlikely that either of them could be wrong, and quite impossible that they both could. What is troubling you?'

'Well – the cost.' Joanna flushed. 'Sir Oscar insists

that the work must be so intensive that he refuses to let me even look for a job. And although my mother and I would naturally have expected to contribute towards the fees, something disastrous has happened at this vital moment. You've heard of the Home and Overseas crash?'

'Yes, indeed!' From his grim expression she conjectured that friends of his in the district had probably been among the substantial losers Aunt Georgina had mentioned.

'Well, I'm afraid Mother lost a frightful amount of money in that and I can't even tell her I need extra money at this moment. She couldn't hope to raise it and would be heartbroken that I should have to refuse this unique chance.'

'Yes, I see.' He looked grave but did not, she noted with embarrassed dismay, immediately offer to implement any promises of help which he had mentioned earlier.

'Sir Oscar suggested—' she cleared her throat nervously – 'he said you had been good enough to offer to help financially if I should need it. And I – I thought you wouldn't mind my coming and telling you about the situation—'

Her voice trailed away and she wondered if it were only her miserable self-consciousness which made her think the slight pause of some significance.

'My dear child, of course I'll help.' He spoke with considerable firmness when he did reply. 'Do you know how much is involved?'

'N-not yet.' Joanna choked slightly in her overwhelming relief. 'Madame Volnikov was going to write to Sir Oscar. He is the one who has the overall direction of the plan.'

'I'll get in touch with him tomorrow – or perhaps even this evening,' Mr. Wilmore promised. 'Now why on earth are you crying, you silly girl?'

'I'm not crying – really.' Joanna fumbled for her handkerchief and dabbed her eyes. 'It's silly, I know. But I felt awful asking, and now the relief—'

And at that moment Sara came sauntering round the corner of the tall yew hedge and stopped short at the sight of them.

'Uncle Justin, what *are* you doing? – reducing your visitor to tears!'

'Nothing of the kind,' retorted Mr. Wilmore, rather brusquely for him. 'And what are *you* doing, out here without a coat? If your cold was sufficiently severe to keep you away from the theatre you certainly shouldn't be wandering about the garden on a chilly afternoon without a wrap.'

'You're right, as always.' She leaned forward and gave him the lightest of kisses, and then turned obediently towards the house, an odd little smile on her lips.

'I'll phone Warrender at the first opportunity,' Mr. Wilmore promised, taking up the conversation where Sara had interrupted it. 'And I think I can promise that everything will be arranged satisfactorily.'

'You're so wonderfully good and generous! I hardly know what to say.' Joanna's smile was still a trifle tremulous. 'But I want you to know that what I'm asking for is a loan. If I do justify everyone's hopes and eventually score a success, I should want to return the money at the first opportunity.'

'We'll see about that when the time comes.' He laughed indulgently and, taking her by the arm, walked back with her to the house, where tea was just being brought into the drawing-room.

Here Sara joined them, of course. And although she made herself pleasant, and even asked interested questions about Joanna's career, it was impossible not to feel vaguely uncomfortable in her presence, and to be glad when it was time to go.

In the hall, where Mr. Wilmore took the kindest leave of her, Joanna earnestly impressed on him the necessity for secrecy about the whole project until plans were much further forward. Then, after a brief call once more on Aunt Georgina, she caught an early evening bus home, feeling that, agitating though certain aspects of her visit had been, she could now venture to look into the future with more confidence than she had felt for some time.

As she let herself into the house her mother came out into the hall, and announced with an air of satisfaction that Elliot Cheam had telephoned only ten minutes ago.

'I promised you would call back if you arrived home within an hour.'

'Elliot Cheam?' An unexpected thrill of pleasure and excitement warred for a moment with the familiar sense of uneasiness which she associated with him whenever she had been anywhere near his uncle. 'What did he want?'

'I think he wanted you to meet him for dinner somewhere.'

'Did he?' Again that wave of elation. 'What for?'

'What *for*?' repeated her mother. 'For the pleasure of your company, I suppose, you funny girl. Why does an attractive young man usually ask a nice girl to dine with him?'

'There are quite a number of reasons,' replied Joanna, but she was smiling happily. 'As I told you, he's deeply involved with his leading lady—' Then she stopped and, for the first time, wondered if there had been something more than a mild indisposition behind Sara's visit to Wilmore Manor.

She went to the telephone without another word and dialled Elliot's number.

'Elliot Cheam,' said his voice. 'Is that Joanna?'

'Yes. How did you know?'

'I'm psychic,' he said. And when she laughed he added, an unusually persuasive note in his voice, 'Are you too tired after your journey to come out to dinner with me?'

'No, of course not.' Joanna was suddenly aware that she had never felt less tired in her life. 'Who told you I'd been on a journey?'

'Your mother. You've been to see Aunt Georgina, and also my uncle, I understand. How did you find him?'

Nothing could have been more normal than the tone of his question, and the complete absence of that all-too-familiar suspicion in his voice warmed her heart as nothing – and she realized suddenly, *nothing* – else could have done.

'He was in fine form, and just as kind as always. I'll tell you about it.' As she said the words she knew of course that she could tell him absolutely nothing of significance about their conversation. 'Would you like me to meet you somewhere or—?'

'No. I'll collect you in half an hour. Does that suit you?'

She said it did, and then rang off and stood there smiling for a moment, in such a mood of happy reflection that her mother, hearing absolute silence after the replacing of the receiver, called out, 'Is everything all right, dear?'

'Oh, yes, Mother.' She came and stood in the sitting-room doorway. 'It couldn't be more all right!' And then, without waiting to enlarge on that, she dashed upstairs to change into the prettiest dress she possessed.

She was ready when he arrived. And his first glance, though it passed over her briefly, told her that she had chosen well. He exchanged a few gay, bantering remarks with her mother, and then he and Joanna went off together.

As on that first occasion, he asked her if there were any special place she would like to choose, and this time she answered without hesitation, 'The same place as before, please.'

'Why?' He looked amused.

'Because it's a lovely place, and because I met the Warrenders there, and because for the first time you gave me the impression that perhaps you were not going to dislike me after all.'

'All excellent reasons,' he admitted with a laugh. 'And, à propos the Warrenders, did he ever let you know what he thought of your Fiora?'

'Oh – oh, yes.' She was faintly startled to find herself immediately so near the forbidden subject. 'He telephoned the next day and congratulated me. I think he still found my acting more interesting than my singing.'

'Did he?' Elliot shot her an interested glance. 'Well, it's of quite a high order, I would say. But you have to remember that speaking a part is a very different matter from singing it.'

'I'm sure it is,' Joanna said earnestly, and changed the subject by saying, 'Speaking of real actresses, Sara

Fernie was at Wilmore Manor when I looked in there.'

'Oh – was she?' He smiled a trifle grimly and, to her surprise, pursued the matter no further until they were seated opposite each other at the same table as before. Then he asked, as he studied the menu, 'And what had Sara to say about me?'

'About *you?*' Joanna looked surprised. 'She didn't mention you. She and I are not quite on those terms, you know.'

'No, I don't know. What sort of terms do you mean?'

'I don't think she would honour me with any girlish confidences. What's the matter? Have you quarrelled again?'

He didn't answer that immediately. Then, without looking up, he said, 'I tried out your theory. The theory that with the Sara type of girl it's healthy to display some indifference if she starts to play up.'

'Oh?' Joanna sounded doubtful. 'And did it work?'

'Depends what you mean by working, my dear.' He did look up then. 'She made me pretty wild about something – it doesn't matter what, but it involved my authority at the theatre – and so I put on a splendid display of indifference.'

'With what result?' Joanna looked amused.

'With the result that suddenly I found I was not putting on a display at all. Quite simply, I *was* indifferent. The spell was somehow broken.'

'But not just because you'd been feigning indifference?' Joanna was very slightly shocked. 'One's emotions don't work like that. At least, only if they're skin-deep. And I don't think your feelings for Sara were just skin-deep, were they?'

'No.' He shook his head. 'I was quite crazily in love with her at one time. Uncritically in love, I suppose you could say. It went on even after I began to see things about her that didn't fit into my picture of her. This latest upset wasn't the first row we had had, by a long chalk. I thought the familiar pattern would repeat itself and that we would make it up. But when I stood back from the scene, as you might say, while I built up my pretence of indifference, I suddenly – no, perhaps it was gradually – saw that, somewhere along the road, I had lost the real feeling. I was just going through the motions. The indifference was not a pretence. It was a natural expression of what my true feelings had become.'

'I see,' said Joanna slowly. 'Do you want me to commiserate with you on losing an ideal or congratulate you on losing your chains?'

'Oh, congratulate me,' he retorted lightly. 'The sense of freedom is almost intoxicating. I had to celebrate it in some way; that's why I asked you to dinner. You seemed to be the natural person to share the celebration.'

'*I* did?' She sounded a little indignant. 'I don't specialize in rescuing besotted young men.'

At that he laughed so much that she could not help smiling too. He was so extraordinarily handsome when he threw back his head like that and his eyes sparkled with amusement.

'You have the most wonderful turn of phrase at times,' he declared. 'That's one reason why you're such a delightful companion.'

'Am I that?' She smiled slightly into her glass, because all at once it was a little difficult to meet his eyes.

'Of course, darling,' he said. And she knew that this was not a casual 'darling' – the type of endearment that was bandied about so easily between people in his world. This time he *meant* it. She *was* a darling to him. And the thought warmed her very heart and made the whole world a lovely place to live in.

She wished she could have told him about the other wonderful things which had happened to her in the last few days. The incredible offer from Oscar Warrender, the unbelievable things Madame Volnikov had said to her; even, in that expansive moment, all about the visit to his uncle and the superb, characteristic generosity with which he was prepared to make the whole miracle work.

But then she remembered how essential it was that all this should remain secret for a while longer from even her nearest and dearest. And as that phrase formed in her mind she gave a small, almost inaudible gasp, for yet anothing shining discovery opened out before her. Elliot was her nearest and dearest.

Small though the gasp was, he must have heard it, for he asked softly, 'What's the matter, Joanna?'

She shook her head.

'Nothing is the matter. Everything is – is wonderful.'

'Is it?' He reached for her hand as it lay on the table and imprisoned it in his. 'Tell me why everything is wonderful.'

'Oh—' She glanced up quickly then, and realized that she had to give some sort of explanation for her impulsive words. She could not say, 'I've just discovered that I'm in love with you.' She could not even say, 'What did you mean when you called me "darling" in that special tone of voice?'

146

And then it came to her that perhaps she could legitimately tell him of one aspect of her dramatically changed fortunes. Something that would account for her air of suppressed excitement, and her inability to conceal the magic of her present mood. She could not tell him much, of course. Her promise to the intimidating Oscar Warrender prevented that. But she could mention just one thing, in a general sort of way. And so she smiled at him with eager candour and said,

'I've been longing to tell someone! And, since you've said such nice things about me, I'm going to tell *you*. But it's a secret for the moment, Elliot. Promise!'

'I promise.' He looked intrigued.

'Have you ever heard of Tamara Volnikov?'

'Of course – the dancer. What about her?'

'She's going to give me lessons – in mime and acting and general stage training. Oscar Warrender is arranging it. He thinks I'm worthy of such lessons.'

'*Warrender* thinks so?' Elliot looked incredulous and, for some reason, not entirely pleased. 'Is he paying?' he asked abruptly.

'No,' she asserted steadily. 'He's getting some wealthy patron of the arts to do that.'

'It's going to have to be a pretty wealthy patron to satisfy that old cormorant. Is it anyone you know personally?'

'No,' lied Joanna coolly, though by now she was wishing she had never embarked on this conversation.

'You know why I'm asking, don't you?'

'No.' She shook her head, and Volnikov herself could not have looked more candid and innocent.

'Because the man who will pay out that sort of money usually wants something in return.'

'Don't be an idiot!' In her relief at his failure to make the obvious guess she actually laughed convincingly. 'How do you know it's a man? It may be a woman, for all I know. Anyway, I'm leaving that to Sir Oscar. — And don't you go asking him questions! He'd kill me if he thought I had so much as breathed a word to you or anyone else.'

'Why?' asked Elliot flatly.

'Why?' She groped again for a convincing reply. 'Because he has some idea of following his own hunch about me, I suppose, but wouldn't like it if I proved him wrong. Isn't that rather the way Oscar Warrender ticks?'

'Ye-es, I suppose it is.' Elliot was more than half convinced now, she saw, and insensibly both of them relaxed, like two adversaries who suddenly realized there was little reason for them to measure up to each other after all. 'I'm very glad for your sake, my dear,' he said much more gently. 'But you understand why I had to ask those questions, don't you?'

'Not really,' she replied lightly. 'After all, I'm not exactly your concern, am I?'

There was quite a long pause.

'You mean it's too quick a change-round if I say that I wish you *were* my concern?' he said at last. 'I've hardly convinced you of my indifference to Sara and here I am trying to make you regard me as something special in your life. Is that it?'

'Not entirely, Elliot.' She glanced down at their clasped hands, and tried to find the right words. There was something in what he had just said, of course. There was even more in the difficulty of believing in the discovery she had just made about her own feelings. But most of all was the thought that for some months at any rate she was going to have to live a sort of secret life. The most important thing in her whole career was opening up before her. If she gave him some sort of right to share in her thoughts and experiences how was she to maintain the secrecy which had been so sternly enjoined upon her?

Luckily or unluckily, they were interrupted at that moment by the waiter bringing their meal. And by the time they had disengaged hands, and the dishes had been set on the table, a slightly more prosaic mood inevitably prevailed.

'All right—' he smiled across at her when they were once more alone. 'Let's not rush our fences. Forget the exact words if you prefer to, and just remember that all the questions I asked were dictated by the fact that you and your future matter quite a lot to me. Does that fit the mood of the moment?'

'Perfectly!' Her smile was as gay and warm as his, 'And I'm glad that you said *all* you did.'

'Darling!' Again the endearment held more than a casual meaning. 'Now tell me about your visit to Volnikov. Didn't she terrify you?'

So Joanna gave him a lively account of her first encounter with the legendary dancer, taking care to keep it all in general terms, and not for one moment suggesting that the training was intended for a specific project.

It was all rather easy, once she had embarked on a perfectly true description of the actual visit, and they both laughed a good deal together, and at the same time he showed a genuine respect for her artistic comments.

'There always seems something new to discover about you, Joanna,' he said when he took her home.

And as he said good night to her he suddenly drew her into his arms and kissed her.

There was nothing casual about the kiss, any more than there had been about the twice he had called her 'darling'. And as Joanna kissed him in return she was aware that this probably betrayed her true feelings far more than any words could have done.

He would have detained her a moment longer, his arms very close around her. But she broke away from him with a breathless little laugh which she tried to make lighthearted instead of excited. Then she ran up the short path to her front door and let herself in without once looking back at him.

It was late and her mother was already in bed, so that the house was very quiet as she leant against the door and drew one or two quick breaths, while her heart beat loudly in the stillness.

'It's true!' she told herself. 'It really happened. Oh, I'm so *happy*! All this – and Sir Oscar's plans as well. It's almost too much. And Mr. Wilmore's generosity too. I don't know what I've ever done to deserve it all.'

During the next week or two the eager dreams were translated into sober fact. Neither Volnikov nor Oscar Warrender could be described as indulgent. Both could inspire one to an extraordinary degree, but Joanna soon found that their demands on her understanding, her capacity for work and her sheer stamina were formidable.

'Tears have a place in every artist's development,' the old Russian dancer observed, when she had actually reduced Joanna to tears one day. 'But beyond a certain point they are an emotional indulgence. It is the *unshed tears* which move an audience to the depths.' And in some strange and magical way she began to channel Joanna's frequent despair and protest into gesture and facial expression.

Warrender came more brutally to the point, when he gave her a gruelling lesson on the final aria in her otherwise silent role. He simply said, 'Stop sniffing and gulping. The one interferes with the purity of tone and the other spoils your phrasing. Now try that again.'

Quite simply, both took perfection as the norm, and any deviation from that standard irritated them. There were moments in those first two or three weeks when Joanna wondered why on earth she had taken on this impossible challenge. But there were also moments when she glimpsed what was required of her, and the few almost grudging words of praise vouchsafed her on those occasions elated her as nothing else had ever done in her whole life before.

Nothing, that was to say, except the discovery that she loved Elliot and that he was not indifferent to her.

She saw very little of him during that first week or two. Unexpectedly he had to fly to the States to discuss the New York production of a play in which he was interested. And for this Joanna was almost glad. For nothing and no one must distract her from her present work, and if she had been seeing Elliot frequently it was hard to see how she could have maintained a discreet silence about the project on which her every hope and effort was fixed.

About this time she met the composer of the work which occupied so much of her time and thought. He was a kind, mild-mannered man, and in startling contrast to the star quality which blazed from both Volnikov and Warrender, his almost gentle and deprecating way of speaking to Joanna made her doubly determined to make a success of his work if it were humanly possible.

'One can never quite assess one's own work until one hears it performed,' he told her. 'But now that I've heard you sing that air – and sing it so beautifully, my dear – I feel that, unpractical though the work may be in some ways, it could indeed have a future.'

'Sir Oscar is sure of it,' Joanna declared. 'And, in my opinion for what it's worth, it is an utterly lovely work. At first, like everyone else, I thought that a whole evening of virtual silence would be impossible to sustain. But with Madame Volnikov's help I'm sure I can do it.'

'You really gather inspiration from that unlikeable woman?' Bernard Fulroyd smiled at her doubtfully and, taking off his spectacles, polished them vigorously – a trick he had when he was either moved or nervous. 'I confess she terrifies me.'

'Well, she terrifies me sometimes,' Joanna conceded with a laugh. 'But she is a unique teacher, and if I make any success of this role it will be due to her. And Sir Oscar, of course.'

'Ah, Sir Oscar! There's a man!' said Mr. Fulroyd. 'I owe him more than I could possibly say. I doubt if any of my music would have reached public performance without his help. He seems confident he'll put this work on the stage. Indeed, he was telling me this morning that, if his plans for the backing turn out as he is expecting, we might look forward to a first night in less than six months' time.'

'He said *that*?' Joanna's eyes shone and the colour rushed into her cheeks. 'Then he must think I'm shaping all right.'

'I think he's very pleased indeed with you,' replied

Mr. Fulroyd. Which was more than Joanna had dared to hope, for the conductor had been sparing indeed with his praise.

She went home after that talk with her spirits high. But, at the same time, the mention of a first night within the foreseeable future seemed to bring the whole enterprise into clear – and terrifying – perspective. So far, her ambition had been merely to satisfy Warrender and the old Russian dancer. From day to day that had been the limit of her effort.

Now, however, when the composer himself appeared to be looking forward with some confidence to hearing his work performed, she realized with a great bump of her heart the tremendous weight of responsibility which was going to rest upon her. If, as Warrender himself had said, she was uniquely suitable for this role – a role that few singers either could or would take on – she was more or less essential to the whole project.

'*I* have to make that dear man's work a success!' Joanna thought. 'I could also make it fail. But I mustn't even think of failure. I must just work hard, and believe that my star is riding high. And it is, it is! Oh, I wonder when Elliot is coming home from the States.'

She had been walking the last part of the journey home, which she did most days as an antidote to the hours she spent in concentrated study, and as she turned into her road she saw, with an uprush of joy, that a familiar car stood outside her home.

'Elliot!' She broke into a run. And then when she came up to the car she saw he was sitting in the driving seat still and had apparently not made any attempt to go into the house. 'Elliot, how wonderful!' She bent down to speak to him through the window. 'Why didn't you knock and go in?'

'I did knock.' He got out of the car and gave her a slight smile, though he did not attempt to kiss her, perhaps because it was broad daylight which hardly contributed to a romantic mood. 'But I think your mother must be out.'

'She is – I remember. She was going to a matinée with a friend. But come on in.' She led the way up the path and opened the door. 'I'll give you tea. Oh, I'm so *glad* to see you, Elliot. Did everything go well in the States?'

'Yes. And—' she suddenly thought he was speaking with some sort of effort – 'is everything going well with you too?'

'Yes, of course. I'll get tea.' She bent to switch on the fire, and as she came upright again he caught her lightly by the arm.

'No – wait a moment.'

She stood still and said in surprise, 'Is something wrong?'

'I don't know. No – I hope not. But I have to ask you something, Joanna. I *have* to ask you, will you believe me? And if I'm doing you an injustice, try to forgive me.'

She said nothing. Only stood there close beside him, with his hand still on her arm.

'Well?' she said at last, aware that her lips had gone dry.

'Joanna, is it my uncle who's paying for your lessons with Volnikov?'

She felt a little as though the floor had opened up in front of her. In a way, she would have been glad if it had, so long as she could have disappeared in some magical way from this terrible moment. But there was no escape. He was holding her arm fast, and he was looking at her with an almost pleading expression which, even as she stared back at him, began to change to one of cold anger.

'Yes,' she said at last. 'But you must let me explain—'

'There's nothing *to* explain!' he interrupted violently. 'It's perfectly simple. You wanted those lessons and so you went crying to him—'

'I did not go crying to him! And I'm sure he never told you any such thing. The fact was—'

'Sara told me,' he said flatly. 'She saw you clinging to him and crying in the garden. And she overheard you asking him for money.'

'It wasn't like that at all!' she cried angrily. 'He had always said – offered—'

'I don't care how it was.' Suddenly his voice was cold and extremely well controlled. 'There are no circumstances which could make it anything but contemptible. Do you know what he did, so that he could satisfy your inexcusable demands? He started to sell some of his collection – the things he loved—'

'Oh, no, no, no. It's not true,' she cried wildly. 'He *couldn't* do any such thing. Why should he? What possible need could there be for that? He's quite a wealthy—'

'He lost heavily in that crash of the Home and Overseas Company. He'd have had to economize sharply in any case. And at just that moment, along you came snivelling for money to pay for these ridiculous lessons with that old Russian vulture. You make me sick, you little – gold-digger!'

He flung the word at her, and at the same moment

he released his grip on her, so that she actually staggered back against the wall.

'Elliot, listen to me! I didn't know – I hadn't the slightest idea! How could I? Please believe me when I say—'

But he brushed past her as though he hardly saw her and went out of the room. Two seconds later she heard the front door close, and she was alone in the house. Alone with her shattered dreams and a horrified sense of remorse.

CHAPTER EIGHT

For several moments Joanna stood there, just where Elliot had left her, crushed by a complete sense of disaster and grief which seemed to encompass all the reasons for her wretchedness. Remorse for what she had done to Mr. Wilmore, anguish because of Elliot's fury, and despair at the way her hopes were crashing in ruins.

But slowly there sifted to the top of her consciousness the thing which gave her most agony. Mr. Wilmore, who had never been anything but kind and generous and understanding, had started to sell his precious treasures because she – *she* – had gone and asked him for money.

Shame and remorse engulfed her at the thought, and she actually gave a little groan of distress as she told herself she had been guilty of that most contemptible of all reactions – ingratitude.

'I must stop it!' She spoke aloud in her misery. 'He mustn't go on with this. Whatever he's sold he must somehow get back. If I never have another lesson in my life, I am not going to have things paid for that way.'

Still trembling with the shock of revelation, she almost tottered to the telephone and unsteadily dialled the number of Wilmore Manor. There was quite a long silence, and then the precise tones of Mrs. Trimble replied.

'Mrs. Trimble—' somehow she steadied her voice – 'please could I speak to Mr. Wilmore?'

'I'm sorry, Miss Joanna. That *is* Miss Joanna, isn't

it? He left home yesterday, and I'm not expecting him back for some time.'

'Can you tell me where he's gone?' Joanna tried to make her voice sound clear and not hoarse with urgency.

'I'm afraid I can't. He'll be travelling round, visiting friends, and I haven't got a forwarding address for the moment. I think he had some idea of joining a friend who goes yachting in the Mediterranean. Someone who shares his interest in collecting. It will do him good to get away a bit. He has been just a trifle depressed lately.'

Joanna wanted desperately to ask if the friend with his yacht in the Mediterranean might be the sort of person who would buy treasures from Mr. Wilmore's collection. But her courage failed her. She said something about writing, and hoping her letter could be forwarded, and then she rang off and stood staring at the telephone, wondering what else she could do.

Perhaps, if she could not reach Mr. Wilmore, she might do something from the other end. She started resolutely to dial Oscar Warrender's number. But then she stopped, realizing that it would be quite impossible to explain things to the famous conductor on the telephone. She would have to see him. He was going to take a good deal of personal convincing that his cherished plans must be abandoned.

She left a note for her mother on the hall table, explaining that she had had to go out once more. Then she went out into the street again and, because she felt a terrible sense of urgency now, she took a taxi. Only when she was in it, driving westward, did she reflect bitterly that, in a sense, it was Mr. Wilmore's money she was wasting. The money he had produced from the sale of his treasures.

She felt a few tears trying to force their way between her lashes, but she controlled them somehow. Tears were not going to do her much good if she needed to impress Oscar Warrender.

Never before had she presumed to go to the Warrender apartment without a specific summons, and she felt little less than a trespasser as she pressed the bell and stood outside, waiting in barely-controlled trepidation. Then, quite unexpectedly, it was Warrender himself who opened the door, which almost robbed her of the few words she had prepared.

'Can I come in, please?' she said timidly. 'S-something has happened, and I have to see you about it.'

'Well then – come in.' He stood aside for her and told her to go into the studio, which at least was reasonably familiar ground to her. Then he followed her in, told her to sit down and, to her surprise, asked her if she felt in need of a brandy.

'Oh, no, thank you!' Joanna wondered for the first time how sick she looked. 'But perhaps a strong coffee if – if—'

He rang the bell and ordered a strong coffee. Then he simply waited for her to speak.

'It's about – the money,' she got out at last.

'What money?'

'The money Mr. Wilmore has been giving for my lessons. It must stop. *They* must stop. I didn't know – but he's been selling things from his collection to raise it.'

'Rubbish,' said Warrender imperturbably. 'And nothing – I repeat *nothing* – must put a stop to your lessons. – Ah, here's your coffee. Drink it up and stop talking nonsense. And then you can explain to me what all this is about.'

She drank the coffee obediently. It was hot enough to burn her mouth slightly, but she was almost glad of that because it partially offset the greater anguish in her mind. Then she put down her cup, rattling it slightly in the saucer because her hand was still unsteady, and she said more calmly,

'What I said is quite true, Sir Oscar. I had no idea, but apparently Mr. Wilmore dropped a great deal of money in the recent Home and Overseas crash. He would have had to economize anyway. But just at that moment I – I went to him and asked him to help me with money for my lessons. He agreed generously and almost instantly, as you well know. It never entered my head that there was any real difficulty. But now I've heard—'

'From Wilmore himself?'

'Oh, no. From—' she swallowed – 'his nephew. There's no question about the facts. His uncle's started to sell—'

'All collectors sell unwanted items from time to time,' said Warrender impatiently. 'They find they have duplicates, or their preferences change and what was once precious seems no longer to be so. Or sometimes items will rise so steeply in value on the market that it seems a good time to sell rather than retain something for sheer sentiment.'

'What Mr. Wilmore chose to do with his collection for personal reasons is no concern of mine.' Joanna was surprised at the firmness of her own voice. 'But he sold because of *my* request, not for any preference of his own. That's the difference.'

'Well then, it seems he valued your artistic progress beyond whatever he sold. What more is there to say?'

returned Warrender shortly.

'Sir Oscar, you're arguing from entirely false premises, and you know it,' stated Joanna, and she was vaguely pleased to see a look of startled annoyance come into his eyes.

He was silent for almost half a minute, then he said slowly,

'No. I'm arguing from what I consider to be the right scale of values. Wilmore presumably made his decision from the same viewpoint. Of course he treasured his collection, certainly to the extent of not selling any of his favourite possessions. But his interest in developing a unique talent was also obviously of worth to him. He balanced one important consideration against another and made his choice.'

'No, he didn't.' She wondered afterwards how she found the courage to go on arguing flatly with the great Oscar Warrender. 'He said "yes" to me because I cried and he hadn't the heart to say "no". That's what I can't accept. That's what makes me feel a cheap cadger. And that's why the whole thing has to stop.'

'What whole thing has to stop?' asked Warrender, in a tone of such dangerous calm that she felt as though someone had hit her under the chin.

'I can't let him pay for any more lessons. I can't continue—'

'The payments have already been arranged. Some of the money has already been passed over. You don't suppose Volnikov is the type to give lessons on credit, do you?' said Warrender brutally. 'You're talking like a child. I tell you the arrangements have all been made—'

'Then they can be unmade, so far as the future is concerned,' she retorted as brutally in her turn.

'Don't be a fool.' The conductor got up and towered over her. 'These lessons – paid for willingly by Wilmore so far as we know – may be a small piece in the jigsaw of the whole enterprise, but they are vital. I dislike giving you an inflated idea of your own importance, but you too are vital to the scheme. A trained and perfected "you" who will need every one of those lessons. Without that, the whole thing falls to the ground. Bernard Fulroyd's humble hopes and ambitions, for instance, will be blasted. Have you thought about that? He isn't a young man. He hasn't got time on his side if he is to see the well-deserved success of his own fine work. If—'

'You're just playing on my sympathies!' cried Joanna defensively, though she was shaken by this argument.

'Of course I'm playing on your sympathies. They and a rich vein of sentimentality seem to be all that's working in you at the moment,' returned Warrender coldly. 'You have no sense of logic or proportion – or loyalty. What about the people who have put their work and their hopes and their faith in you?'

'Oh—' Joanna buried her face in her hands and tried to think clearly and fairly. And what rose before her at that moment was not the kind face of Mr. Wilmore, but the deprecating, eager face of Bernard Fulroyd. 'How can I take the money, knowing what I do?' she muttered helplessly.

'*You* aren't taking it,' Warrender told her cynically. 'Volnikov is taking it – with both hands. We don't know – any of us – just how Wilmore financed and is continuing to finance your training. But the arrangements have been made and must continue. Do you understand? *They must continue*, if all the work

162

and hopes of several people are not to founder.'

'Couldn't we somehow get the money from somewhere else? I mean, whatever money is needed from this point?'

'Not from anywhere I know of,' replied Warrender coolly. 'I have channelled any resources I can myself call on into the actual production and performances. And I assure you I am losing no sleep over any sacrifices my backers may be making. They are responsible adults capable of choosing for themselves. You'd better credit Wilmore with equal sense.'

'It's different,' Joanna protested, but more uncertainly.

'Well, I didn't have to go and cry on anyone's shoulder,' Warrender admitted with a dry smile. 'But the principle is the same. A good many sacrifices go into any worthwhile artistic endeavour. You have to accept that, child. And you'll make some yourself before we are finished.'

She sat there digesting that in silence, and presently she became aware with blinding clarity that of course he was right. What *she* had to sacrifice was Elliot's good opinion of her.

Once she had faced that and, with fearful reluctance, accepted it, the conflict was over. So was the conversation, to all intents and purposes. She got up after a moment or two and said quietly, 'Perhaps you're right. I'm not absolutely sure you are. But I do see that I can't let everyone down now.'

'Sensible girl,' observed Warrender. 'And if it's any consolation to you, Wilmore would be the first to be appalled if you withdrew now and wrecked the whole enterprise. All you can do now for everyone, including Wilmore, is to see that our combined efforts are not wasted.'

'I'll do my best,' said Joanna. And for the first time she realized all that was implied by that promise.

It pursued her, haunted her and, in some strange way, sustained her during the next few months, which were probably the most important and productive of her whole life. Certainly so far as her career was concerned.

The very fact that she was unhappy personally enabled her to sink her identity and all her energies in her artistic life. Here she began to finding an abiding consolation for what she had lost elsewhere. Everything she had been with difficulty absorbing from Tamara Volnikov began at last to make sense and become part of her, and what had been a conscious effort at first now began to be second nature.

She saw and heard nothing of Elliot during this time and, after thinking feverishly of various ways by which she might see him and force him to understand her dilemma better, she abandoned even the hope of ever regaining his friendship or what she had fondly hoped might be his love.

To Mr. Wilmore she wrote a letter, stiffer in its phrasing than she would have wished it to be, but which in part at least explained how she felt about what he was doing for her. She tried to find some balance between dignified gratitude and excessive self-blame but, though she altered the wording many times, she could not be satisfied with the result. In the end she just sealed it up and sent it, hoping to hear from him in terms that would reassure her.

It was many weeks before his reply came, and it was posted from a port of call in southern Italy. He wrote pleasantly about the trip he was making on his friend's yacht, and only at the end did he mention the matter which had caused her so much anguish.

'There is no need for you to worry about the money for your lessons, my dear,' he wrote in a postscript. 'I seldom paid anything more willingly, and I do assure you that no absolute treasure in my collection had to be sacrificed to this worthy cause.'

With that she had to be satisfied. She *was* satisfied to a great extent, at least so far as he was concerned. Only it did nothing whatever, of course, to restore respect or good feeling between her and Elliot.

There was no one to whom she could confide her inmost thoughts, least of all to her mother, who was beginning to revive after the shock of her financial disaster. To Warrender she had said all that could be said to an outsider and, although as the weeks passed she became almost fond of the hard but fascinating old artist who directed her stage studies, she knew that Volnikov would not even have been interested in any problem connected with the money which paid her for her marvellous coaching.

Oddly enough, it was Warrender's wife, Anthea, who came nearest to being a confidante. Coming on Joanna one afternoon when she was waiting in the studio for Warrender who had been delayed, she exclaimed, 'You sometimes look so sad these days, Joanna. This role isn't getting you down in some way, is it? I mean – are you living it so wholeheartedly that you actually suffer with the character?'

'It could be,' Joanna smiled slightly. 'And if so, it wouldn't be a bad thing, artistically, would it?'

'Well, no,' Anthea agreed. 'That's part of being a real artist, of course. But don't get depressed about your work. You're doing so well. Even Oscar was excited today when he was talking of the work going into production next month.'

'Was he?' Even now there was a sort of unreality about being able to cause excitement to an old hand like Oscár Warrender, and Joanna's smile deepened. 'I'm not worried, Anthea. There's a sort of confidence growing in me – an awareness that I've passed right out of the student stage, to the artist who understands what work and inspiration really mean.'

'The biggest hurdle in any career,' Anthea assured her. 'So don't let any personal issue worry you at this moment, if you can help it. Unless, of course, you can somehow identify it with the role you are going to play.'

'How do you mean?' Joanna glanced at the other girl quickly.

'Well, throughout this work you are playing the part of someone who has to remain silent and be misjudged. Sometimes that happens in one's own life.'

'You're a witch!' Joanna laughed protestingly.

'No. Oscar told me a little and I did a bit of inspired guessing,' Anthea confessed. 'I may have got it wrong, and you don't need to confide in me. But time is a strange thing, Joanna. There are few people who haven't thought at one point or another that nothing can ever come right again. But it has a habit of doing so. I know. It happened with me and Oscar. And speaking of him, I think that's the sound of his key in the door.'

She smiled at Joanna and went out of the room, pausing only for a moment to kiss her husband as she passed him in the doorway.

Whether or not this conversation had anything to do with it, from that day Joanna slipped finally and completely into the part of the silent girl who could not sing of her love until the moment before she died.

Both Warrender and Volnikov had praise for her at last. Not excessive praise. But the kind of heart-warming, professional praise which made her feel, however humbly, at one with those two great artists themselves.

And this was the mood in which she faced the ordeal of the opening rehearsals.

By now, of course, a good deal was being written about the coming performance in the musical pages of most newspapers. But though photographs and interviews were requested, they were arbitrarily refused by Warrender, and Joanna remained almost insulated against the growing interest and excitement which inevitably surrounded any enterprise personally undertaken by Oscar Warrender.

She was glad of it. She preferred to remain immersed in her work, though she did permit herself some faint hope that Elliot might read about it all and perhaps understand a little better why there had been the necessity to accept — no, she must be accurate: to *ask* for — his uncle's financial aid.

But no word came.

'I think it's stupid not to have you photographed,' her mother complained. 'You're the *heroine* of this opera. There's a photograph here of the composer. He looks a nice old gentleman, but no one would call him romantic. Whereas you, a lovely girl, even if I say it myself, about to spring to fame in a night—'

'I haven't sprung yet, Mother. Give me time,' said Joanna, smiling. 'We don't want people talking about me before I've done anything.'

'I should have thought that would make good publicity beforehand,' retorted her mother.

'There's quite enough publicity – don't worry. It comes from interest in a new work and the fact that Sir Oscar is involved in it. And the tenor, Nicholas Brenner, is one of the most famous in the world.'

'Oh, the *tenor*!' exclaimed Mrs. Ransome, in a tone which would have surprised – not to say affronted – most tenors. 'I want to have people inquiring about *you*. Which reminds me, we never see anything of Elliot Cheam these days. What has become of him?'

'I believe he is in the States,' replied Joanna with admirable composure. 'When we last met he was very much taken up with a possible production in New York. I've been so busy myself that I haven't seen anyone much, as you know, and I suppose it's the same with him. That's the theatre world for you!' And she smiled at her mother.

'Well, I expect it will be worth it all in the end. I've just heard from Georgina, by the way, and she's coming to town for the first night. Absolutely insists on it. She spoke on the phone as though she had been responsible for a lot of your career. I can't imagine why. She only got you an introduction to nice Mr. Wilmore.'

'Perhaps,' said Joanna slowly, 'that *was* the beginning of it all. Anyway, I'd like Aunt Georgina to be there.'

'But not sitting absolutely beside me, dear, I do beg,' exclaimed her mother feelingly. 'Just in case you don't make quite the success everyone is hoping,' she added naïvely.

Just in case you don't make quite the success everyone is hoping. The words stayed somewhere in the depths of Joanna's mind and surfaced uneasily at various moments during the final rehearsals.

Not that she did not receive both encouragement and support from her immediate colleagues. Some of them – like Nicholas Brenner and his wife – declared themselves fascinated by the way she surmounted the difficulties of a largely silent part. But the undoubted fact was that the work itself was almost experimental, and no one could really foretell what its effect would be on the first night audience.

'No one except that wily old devil Warrender, that is to say,' declared Jonathan Keyne, the husband of Mr. Fulroyd's daughter, Anna. 'Trust him to produce exactly the right person for the role. How did he *find* you, Joanna?'

'I came on her by chance – if these things *are* chance,' said the wily old devil, coming up behind Jonathan Keyne at that moment. 'And I backed my own instinct and judgment. Don't praise her any further. She has yet to prove herself finally.'

But he put his hand lightly on Joanna's shoulder. And, because it was a very expressive hand indeed, she knew he was satisfied with her, and she went home from the dress rehearsal in an almost tranquil frame of mind.

This mood of tranquillity did not of course persist for any real length of time. In the hurrying yet crawling hours until the actual performance Joanna alternated between hope and despair, the belief that everything was going to be wonderful and the certainty that shame and disaster lay ahead. Oddly enough, her mother was quite a support during this difficult time, for her capacity for goodhumoured but trivial chatter kept Joanna from sinking too far or riding too high on the emotional switchback of those final hours.

By the time she left for the Opera House on the great night itself she found she was almost calm. But whether or not this was the calmness of despair she would not have liked to say.

On arriving in her dressing-room, she was surprised and a little put out to find Madame Volnikov there, waiting for her, and looking much more the heroine of the evening, in her Russian sables, than Joanna did. In the first moment she supposed she was to receive some last-minute instructions, but the famous old dancer merely smiled her beautiful smile, drew herself up as though for a ceremonial occasion and said,

'Until now, Joanna, I have been sparing in my praise lest you should rest too easily on your immature laurels. But tonight it is right you should know that you have satisfied my highest expectations. You have supplied the instinct without which no artist can even begin. I have supplied the unrivalled training without which no artist can come to full flower. You English have a peculiar phrase – Go in and win. I say this to you now, for *you cannot fail.*'

She then kissed the astonished and moved Joanna and took her departure. As she went out a handsome bouquet was handed in and, a little dazed still, Joanna examined the accompanying card. She saw, with the utmost pleasure, that it was from Mr. Wilmore, and the note bore not only the expression of his affectionate good wishes, but the information that he would be in the house that night.

It was the last touch needed to spur her to highest endeavour. This was her supreme chance to make him feel that his generous sacrifice had indeed been worthwhile.

When Warrender came to have a last word with her

before the performance began, he found her sitting before her dressing-table, outwardly very calm and already wearing the strangely beautiful green and blue costume, with its floating draperies, which gave her such an other-worldly air.

'All right?' He smiled at her briefly.

'Perfectly all right. Except for a sort of fluttering – here.' She put her hand against her breast.

'Every real artist feels nervous on such an occasion,' he said, and the slight emphasis on 'real' was heartening. 'But remember I am there to support you – and I have a strong hand in these matters.'

'I know it.' She returned his smile. 'Thank you for everything, Sir Oscar.'

'Thank me after the performance,' he replied. But he touched her hair lightly before he left her.

She had never before received a gesture of such kindliness and reassurance from him, and for a moment she thought she knew why Anthea was a happy woman. It must be wonderful to know with certainty that the right person loved and understood one. Her part – on the stage tonight and in a more personal way too – was to remain silent and *endure*, whatever the provocation might be. But it was the choice she had made, and she was prepared to abide by it.

Which was perhaps why, from the moment of her first entrance, she captured and held the sympathies of the entire audience.

'Self-sacrifice,' wrote one of the more perceptive of the critics next day, 'is a dangerous commodity to handle on the stage. Combined with self-pity it is immediately unendearing. But combined with the kind of inner strength and human dignity given to it last night by Joanna Ransome it becomes the strongest link possible between performer and audience.'

He was describing, of course, the 'unshed tears' on which Volnikov had insisted. Equally of course, much of the success of Joanna's interpretation was due to the unique lessons she had received from that remarkable woman. What was peculiarly her own contribution however was the fact that she was truly expressing herself, and her own inner conviction. And for most of the evening she merged her identity so completely with the girl she was portraying that it was impossible for her to know herself whether her gestures, her expression and her silent appeal were addressed to Nicholas Brenner, singing the part of her lover like an angel, or – somehow, somewhere in the world – to Elliot who despised her.

The tension – created and sustained throughout the evening by Bernard Fulroyd's beautiful music, the singing of her fellow artists, and her own gripping yet eloquent silence – never faltered. Indeed, one of the stagehands was actually heard to mutter, 'Say something, dearie! just say *something* to him.'

And at the moment when she turned at last to her lover and broke into the beautiful, passionate phrases written for her at that point, not only did Brenner almost literally fall back before her, but throughout the house there ran a sort of shiver of emotion and excitement which exactly paralleled his reaction on the stage.

'It will be the high-point of the performance,' Warrender had told her. 'The challenge is tremendous, for you will have to break into those high, arresting phrases without a shadow of the usual "warming up". On the other hand, all your vocal resources will be fresh and untired. Something,' he added sardonically, 'for which every soprano, from Marguerite to Isolde, would give half her fee at the end of a gruelling performance. Use every bit of vocal technique you possess for that sudden entry. And leave the rest to me.'

He was absolutely right, she found. Those first electrifying phrases came out like the striking of a bell. And then suddenly the compulsion of Warrender's matchless left hand and the expression of his telling face, seen in the light from the orchestra pit, somehow reminded her of everything he had ever taught her about lyrical phrasing, vocal colouring, and perfect diction.

'In a sense,' she afterwards told her mother, 'he almost did it for me.'

This was not quite true, of course. But at least it was the just reward for all the work they had put into it together.

At the end there was the kind of scene beloved of every opera-lover. Just to have been there on such an occasion seemed a triumph to each member of the audience, and so they participated to the full in saluting the great night. The curtain-calls were endless, the applause was thunderous, and finally Warrender pushed Joanna and Bernard Fulroyd on to the stage together.

'Come too! You come too,' they both implored him. But he laughed and shook his head.

'The evening is yours, my dears,' he said. 'Go out and take it.'

So they went out together hand in hand, both of them a little shy and dazed by a reaction neither of them had ever expected to evoke. And each of them — the elderly composer and the very young artist — thought that probably there would never be a moment like this again.

Afterwards, Joanna was engulfed in waves of praise and congratulation from colleagues and friends alike, while her mother and Aunt Georgina glowed with family pride. She cleared the dressing-room temporarily at last. But, just as she was about to close the door, she saw Mr. Wilmore in the corridor and, because she simply could not let him wait for the thanks so richly due to him, she called him in alone, uninhibitedly flung her arms around him and cried.

'Thank you, thank you, thank you! It was you who made it all possible.'

'No, my dear.' A good deal moved, he kissed her and patted her shoulder. 'It was your own tremendous talent and work that made it possible.'

'But all that would have remained undeveloped – useless – without your generosity,' she exclaimed. 'All that money you poured out on me! Sacrificing things you love, never even telling me there were difficulties. I can never—'

'Stop, stop!' Laughingly he put his hand over her eager lips. 'I can't take all this praise. It isn't even wholly mine. I did make the initial payment and, if you like, I was perfectly prepared to pay the rest, even at some sacrifice. But it was not I who paid most of it.'

'It – wasn't?' She stood back from him, staring with wide, astonished eyes. 'Then who was it?'

He gave a slight, embarrassed laugh.

'I was sworn to secrecy, Joanna. But I don't think it can matter now. It was Elliot who provided the bulk of the money.'

CHAPTER NINE

'YOU CAN'T MEAN IT!' Joanna stared at Mr. Wilmore in utter consternation. '*Elliot* paid for my lessons?' It isn't possible!'

'Why not?' Mr. Wilmore looked amused, if a little put out. 'I assure you Elliot is a very generous-hearted fellow under that casual manner of his.'

'But not – to me.' The words were out before she could stop them, and her hands fell to her sides, the fingers curling and uncurling in a gesture as telling as any she had used on the stage.

'What makes you think he would not want to help you?' Mr. Wilmore took one of those restless hands rather gently.

'He doesn't think me worthy of help,' she replied quickly. 'He thinks me a cheap little cadger. And sometimes,' she added with a sigh, 'I wonder if he's right.'

'What nonsense!' Mr. Wilmore spoke with energy. 'You came to me for help, as you might have come to any friend. With special justification, as it happened, because I had already offered my assistance in a general way. There was no question of cadging, and I will not have the word used.'

'*You* wouldn't have it used; you're too generous for that.' She returned the pressure of his hand gratefully. 'But I could hardly have chosen a crueller moment to make my request, from your point of view. That's what shocked Elliot so much.'

'Don't exaggerate.' He brushed her argument aside. 'It was an *awkward* moment, if you like, though you had no means of knowing that. In any case, with care I could have managed. But then Elliot came to me and made his offer; indeed, insisted on finding the money himself.'

'For your sake?' she interjected quickly.

'And yours,' he replied. But there was an infinitesimal pause before he said that, and she thought she knew why.

'Mr. Wilmore, will you please tell me something quite truthfully?' Joanna said earnestly. 'In what mood was Elliot when he first broached the subject to you?'

'In what *mood*?' The fact that he repeated her words told her immediately that he was playing for time, finding the least painful way of telling something approximating to the truth. 'Well, he didn't understand the situation at first, of course. I had to explain things to him. And then he offered, entirely of his own free will, to be of help.'

'Yes, I see.' Joanna spoke gently and resisted any desire to press him further. Why spoil the pleasure of her generous friend by questioning the motive behind what Elliot had done? 'It was very, very kind of – him, and of you. I can never thank you enough.'

She let him suppose that 'you' referred to them both. But she knew now of course, that Elliot's offer had been made solely with the idea of helping his uncle out of an awkward situation which *she* had created.

Then the dresser tapped on the door and put her head in to say rather reproachfully that there were a lot of people waiting.

'I must go.' Mr. Wilmore bent his head and kissed her cheek. 'Thank you, my dear, for a great experience. I think you will find that is how most people will describe tonight.'

They did, of course, when they crowded in once more. At the back of her mind there lingered the extraordinary piece of information about Elliot, but even this was thrust aside in an evening in which Joanna registered some of the strangest and most triumphant moments of her life.

For the first time there was a crowd at the stage door for her. For the first time people asked her for her autograph. For the first time the stage-door keeper had to force a way for her through the throng before he could hand her into the Warrenders' handsome car in which she was driven off to the Gloria for a celebration supper. *Her* celebration supper.

It was quite an intimate party. Just the Warrenders and the Fulroyds, Joanna and her mother and – to her extreme gratification – Aunt Georgina.

Joanna had not met Mrs. Fulroyd before, but she liked her on sight. A quiet, smiling woman who seemed even now faintly surprised at her husband's success. Anna Fulroyd, on the contrary, and her husband, Jonathan Keyne, the producer, seemed to feel that all their confidence in the work had just been triumphantly fulfilled, and they could not praise Joanna enough for her part in making it such a success.

That Joanna's mother and Mrs. Fulroyd should get on well together was to be expected, for each had a talented daughter to talk about. What was more surprising was that Aunt Georgina and Oscar Warrender seemed to strike a certain number of enjoyable sparks from each other's conversation.

'I don't know what has got into my Aunt Georgina,' Joanna murmured to Anthea Warrender. 'She doesn't really know much about the musical world. I shouldn't have expected her and Sir Oscar to have much in common.'

'They have the same rather sardonic sense of humour,' replied Anthea with penetration. 'And the same good-natured contempt for a half-done job. Was she a teacher or something?'

'A formidable headmistress, with a reputation for turning out well-educated girls,' replied Joanna promptly.

'Well, there you are! Oscar is a formidable musical director, with a reputation for turning out properly schooled artists,' said Anthea with a laugh. 'It's the same thing, in a different degree. And, talking of great teachers, Volnikov actually shed a few tears at one point this evening. Did you know?'

'No! How could I? She came afterwards and told me she was pleased, but she said I must work more on the second scene of the first act. And she's right, of course,' Joanna added meditatively.

'Quite right,' observed Warrender, without even turning from Aunt Georgina. 'You made a good start tonight, and you can afford to rest for the whole of to-morrow. But I want you at the studio the following afternoon. There are one or two phrases to polish before Friday night's performance.'

And then the party broke up, and they contentedly went their separate ways, though Mrs. Ransome did observe in the taxi that Oscar Warrender was a slave-driver. 'But an attractive one,' she conceded.

'He's a great man,' said Joanna indignantly.

'He's a sensible man,' said Aunt Georgina, 'which is more important.' Then she yawned prodigiously and added that it had been a very remarkably evening, all told.

As soon as they reached home she went up to bed.

But Joanna and her mother lingered for a few minutes longer, neither of them willing to put an end to this incredible evening. And it was then that Mrs. Ransome said as an afterthought, 'By the way, I saw Elliot Cheam in the house.'

'You – what?' Joanna choked slightly on the word. 'Did you speak to him?'

'No. I was just going over to do so, but he evidently didn't see me. He walked off in the other direction and I lost him in the crowd.'

'I see,' said Joanna. And suddenly she felt that the magic had gone out of the evening. So she said good night to her mother and went upstairs to her bed, where she lay awake and watched the stars through her bedroom window until they began to fade in the first pale light of the morning. And then she fell asleep.

No one woke her next morning until she came to the surface of her own accord. But then, when she looked at the time, she sprang out of bed, her confidence suddenly plummeting, and ran to call her mother.

'Mother, Mother, I'm awake! What do the papers say? Is it – bad, after all?'

Her mother came hurrying up the stairs, a pile of newspapers clutched to her bosom.

'Darling, I was longing to wake you! But Georgina wouldn't let me.' It struck neither of them as strange that Aunt Georgina should tell them what to do in their own house. 'But they're all wonderful! Every single one, except one silly man who says the best singing of the evening came from the tenor.'

'Well, it did,' replied Joanna. 'Brenner carried the vocal weight of the evening and carried it superbly. You must allow him that.'

On her mother's insistence she went back to bed,

where she lay surrounded by the morning's papers, while Mrs. Ransome went down to get her breakfast because, as she said, to this extent at least she intended to treat her daughter as a prima donna.

None of it seemed quite real to Joanna as she read one glowing notice after another. That this was nice Mr. Fulroyd's work they were praising so lavishly seemed quite understandable and just. That Oscar Warrender was said to have conducted superbly and Nicholas Brenner to have added a magnificent portrait to his repertoire – that was quite natural too. But this girl – this unknown girl who had 'virtually disarmed criticism' as one account put it, and enraptured public and critics alike – that this should be herself, Joanna Ransome, was not to be believed.

'It doesn't seem possible, does it?' she said dazedly, as her mother came in with the breakfast tray.

'Not really,' Mrs. Ransome confessed. 'Though of course *I* always knew you had it in you to be famous one day,' she added loyally.

'No, you didn't, Pansy – any more than anyone else,' declared Aunt Georgina, coming in at this moment to say good-bye before going to catch her Green Line bus. 'And don't let all this turn your head, Joanna.' She gestured towards the newspapers on the bed.

'No, Aunt Georgina,' Joanna smiled happily at her.

'Though with that sensible Warrender man, you won't probably have much chance,' she added. 'Nor with that strange old Russian woman. What did *she* really have to do with it, Joanna?'

'Almost everything,' Joanna declared, attacking her breakfast with good appetite. 'Except for what Sir Oscar did, I mean.'

'Well, modesty is always seemly,' said her aunt, as

she dropped a kiss on the top of Joanna's head, 'but don't under-value yourself too sharply. That's just as silly as boasting.'

And on this sensible dictum she took her leave.

Even after she had finished her breakfast, and her mother had gone downstairs again, Joanna lay there, still savouring the incredibility of all that had happened. And then, suddenly, she found that her thoughts were veering round from her triumph to the situation with Elliot.

She would have to see him and thank him for what he had done. Common decency and gratitude demanded that. Equally, self-respect demanded that she should know how much she owed him and assure him that the loan – for loan it must be – would be repaid.

It would not be an easy conversation, wherever it took place. Which brought her round to the simple problem – where *could* it take place? It was not a conversation to be conducted across a restaurant table or in a car. Still less could she ask him to come here to her home. Even supposing she could somehow ensure that her mother was out, it was unthinkable that they should meet again in the room where they had had that last horrible, violent scene of recrimination.

She had never been to his flat, and this was not the moment to insist on making a first visit there. And if she went to the theatre and asked for him he might well not be there, or refuse to see her. Worse still, Sara might somehow wander into the picture.

'But I must find some way,' she told herself. And at that moment her mother called upstairs to say that Anthea Warrender was on the telephone.

Joanna snatched up a wrap and ran downstairs to take the call.

'How do you feel this morning?' Anthea's gay voice inquired, and the lilt of happiness in it showed that she too had read all the favourable notices.

'How did *you* feel, the morning after your first success as Desdemona?' Joanna countered.

'Like heaven,' replied Anthea promptly. 'But then I'd just got engaged to Oscar the night before, so I can't really tell you which was the more thrilling.'

'That must have been – wonderful.' Joanna was unaware of the catch in her own voice. 'Since he was the one man you wanted, I mean.'

'It's a wonderful moment when it happens – as you'll find, my dear, one day,' Anthea declared. 'But I won't stop to speculate now. Here is Oscar to speak to you.'

And then Warrender's deep, pleasant voice said, 'Good morning, starlet. It seems the work was all worthwhile.'

'Oh, Sir Oscar, of course it was! and I can never, never thank you and Madame Volnikov enough.'

'Well, it wasn't all on one side, you know. A pupil who satisfies one's every hope and expectation is a pretty good present to any teacher. You are a good child and earned your success. Also I'm sure Wilmore must think now that his money was very well spent.'

'His—? Oh, he provided only part of it, Sir Oscar. Most of it was provided by Elliot Cheam.'

'Was it, indeed?' Warrender sounded intrigued. 'Who told you that?'

'Mr. Wilmore did. I started to thank him last night, and he explained that in the end it – it was largely Elliot's doing.'

'Very handsome of him,' commented Warrender, on a note of some amusement. 'Whose judgment was he backing, I wonder? Mine or his own?'

'I don't think,' said Joanna diffidently, 'that he was backing anyone's judgment. He just knew his uncle couldn't afford to pay for the lessons, and so he took on the obligation himself.'

'Well, whatever his motive, he did what was necessary.' The conductor sounded altogether too casual about it all, Joanna thought, and she said rather stiffly, 'He was there last night.'

'Did he come round to see you?'

'No.'

There was a pause, and then Warrender said, 'I see.'

'We – quarrelled.' Joanna found herself unable to resist the desire to go on. 'Months ago, I mean. He thought I was cadging from his uncle. We – we haven't seen each other since.'

'Well, you'll have to see him now,' said Warrender's voice bracingly, 'if only to thank him for what he has done.'

'I know. But – how?' Jonna spoke almost to herself.

'*How?*' repeated Warrender, in the tone of one who had never had the slightest difficulty in managing to see anyone he wanted to see. Which was of course the case. 'The usual way, I suppose. Telephone him and say—'

'I couldn't do that,' said Joanna in a rather panic-stricken tone of voice. 'We quarrelled very, very badly, Sir Oscar. A phone call wouldn't do much good.'

'Well, there must be a way. I'll put my mind to it,' Warrender promised, and though he sounded amused it was not unkind amusement. 'When you come to the studio tomorrow afternoon – three o'clock, by the way – I'll have thought of something. You mustn't spoil your triumph with some silly quarrel,'

It was not some silly quarrel, of course. It was a vital and shattering matter. But he was not to know that. And, in any case, she could hardly expect Oscar Warrender to deal with her personal problems. It was enough – more than enough – that he had made her famous.

For the next few hours she entertained the ridiculous hope that Elliot might himself take the initiative and telephone. And every time the phone bell rang – which it did constantly – her hopes soared. But neither then nor the following day was there a word from him.

But when she set off for her lesson the following afternoon her spirits lifted. For achievement is, to a true artist, like a drug; taste it and the desire for more is constant.

The smiling maid who opened the door to her added her congratulations to those of everyone else, and then explained that Sir Oscar had just telephoned to say he had been delayed, and would Joanna mind waiting?

'I don't mind a bit. Is Lady Warrender in?'

'No, Miss Joanna. She's out too. But you go into the studio, and I'll bring you some tea if you like.'

Joanna refused the offer of tea, but she went into the long, beautiful room where so much of her work had been done. Pale sunlight filtered through the curtains, and the greens and golds of Anthea's choice blended like colours in a woodland scene. On the piano was a new and charming photograph of Anthea herself, and Joanna was just studying this with pleasure when the sound of voices in the hall told her that Warrender had returned.

As the door opened, she turned smilingly towards it. But the smile was struck from her face. For the man who came in was not Oscar Warrender. It was Elliot.

'Elliot!' She actually fell back a pace.

'Why – hello!' He looked as astonished as she did, and almost as much put out. 'I had no idea you were going to be here.'

'And I had no idea you were coming. I – I've just come for a lesson.'

'Warrender must have mistaken the time,' he muttered. Then, with an effort, he managed a slight smile and said, 'Do you *need* any lesson after Tuesday night's performance?'

'Yes, of course.' She smiled too, but very nervously. 'It–it was just a good beginning. Were you there, Elliot?'

'Yes, I was there.'

'You didn't feel like coming round to see me?'

'No.' Long pause. 'I didn't think I would be welcome.'

'You would have been,' she said simply. 'And I should have been glad of the opportunity to thank you.'

'Thank me?' He looked unnaturally blank. 'I don't know what you mean.'

'You know perfectly well what I mean.' Her voice shook a little, but she forced herself to go on. 'I started to thank your uncle, and then he told me that it was you who provided most of the money. That's why I have to thank you.'

Perhaps it was an unfortunate choice of words, for he flushed and said, almost aggressively, 'You don't *have* to thank me for anything.'

'I didn't mean it that way! I didn't mean there was any compulsion on me to thank you – though of course there is that too. I – I just *wanted* to thank you. Naturally.'

He stared moodily at the ground and said, 'I

couldn't let my uncle carry the whole burden.'

'Of course not,' she said coldly, because this time *his* choice of words was unfortunate. 'Nor can I let either of you do so indefinitely. As I told your uncle in the beginning, any money was to be considered a loan. And now—' a sort of panic gripped her because all the right words were slipping away from her – 'apart from thanking you for what you advanced, I have to ask you just how much I owe you.'

'You don't owe me anything,' he said harshly, and turned away.

'Of course I do! You don't suppose I would accept an enormous gift of money from you, do you?'

'Why not?' He still had his back to her.

'Because,' she said deliberately, 'I should then be the sort of cadger you've always made me out to be.'

'Oh, forget it!' He swung round to face her again. 'I never meant half the things I said. And anyway—' he stared at the ground again – 'when I saw you the other night I was – glad.'

'Glad of what, Elliot?' Insensibly a little of the hardness had melted from her voice.

'I was glad to have had a hand in – that evening. Oh, you can't buy your way into a great artistic performance, I know. But I sat there thinking, "I did help her in a tiny, unimportant way, after all—"'

He stopped abruptly, and she had the extraordinary impression that he just could not go on.

'It wasn't unimportant, Elliot,' she said at last. 'It was vital. Your generosity—'

'It wasn't generosity!' he exclaimed desperately, and suddenly he dropped into a chair and buried his face in his hands. 'Don't you understand?' his voice came, muffled but so that she could hear every word. 'I'd give anything – *anything* – to be able to say I did it out of generosity to you – the dearest creature in the world. But I didn't. I did it partly from a genuine wish to help my uncle and partly out of pique and arrogance. I thought, "*Let* her have her chance to prove she's no good, and then I'll be free of her." And all the time—'

'Don't, dear! Elliot—' she came and knelt beside him – 'you don't have to say these things.'

'I do have to say them! It's time they were said. There's been too much *un*said. You couldn't say anything, could you? any more than that poor silent girl on the stage. You weren't even allowed to do your own pleading.'

He sat up and looked at her haggardly. Then suddenly he caught her against him so tightly that it hurt.

'When I watched you the other night, telling all your thoughts with the movement of your hands, the turn of your head, the touching expressiveness of your face, it was as though you were speaking to me alone, and telling me what a crass, unknowing brute I'd been.'

'You weren't meant to think that at all,' she murmured in protest, but she also put up a silent prayer of thankfulness to Madame Volnikov.

'Perhaps not. But the message came over so clearly, that I couldn't have stayed in the place except for that small rag of comfort – the thought that I'd helped you with the money, even if from the wrong motives. Please don't take even that away from me, Joanna. Please don't.'

'But I wouldn't take it away from you for the world. Not now,' she said, touching his cheek with a sort of dawning confidence. 'It isn't the moment for taking away, Elliot. It's a moment for giving.'

'Giving?' he repeated, with something between doubt and hope in his voice. 'Giving – what?'

'Reassurance to each other, I suppose. Forgiveness, if that's the word. And then – oh, I don't know what else, except that I love you, and I give you that with all my heart.'

'Joanna—' he passed his hand over her hair again, almost wondering that time – 'is it really as simple as that? That we can say now that we love each other – and the rest is somehow behind us?'

'I don't know what else we should say.' She smiled at him almost mischievously. 'Nothing else matters very much, does it? Except to say thank you for something else that was given to both of us this afternoon. The chance to explain to each other at last.'

'You're right.' He laughed as he kissed her. 'That was a very kind gift of fate, wasn't it?'

'I don't think that was fate,' said Joanna, as she heard a step in the hall. 'I think that was Oscar Warrender. It was thanks to him that you were summoned here at the exact time of my lesson.'

'Nonsense.' Elliot looked amused but unconvinced. 'He just got the times mixed. Wasn't that it?' he added, turning to Warrender as he entered the room. 'You got your appointments mixed, and your timing wasn't too good this afternoon, was it?'

'My timing, my dear fellow,' said the conductor agreeably, 'appears to me to have been absolutely faultless. I invited you here at the hour of Joanna's lesson, in the belief that you would like to hear her at work. You seem to be in the right mood for it. Shall we begin?'

And he went towards the piano.

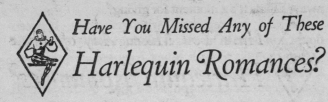

Have You Missed Any of These Harlequin Romances?

All books listed are available at **75c each** at your local bookseller or through the Harlequin Reader Service.

Have You Missed Any of These
Harlequin Romances?

☐ 1857 CRUISE TO A WEDDING, Betty Neels	☐ 1881 THE END OF THE RAINBOW, Betty Neels
☐ 1858 ISLAND OF DARKNESS, Rebecca Stratton	☐ 1882 RIDE OUT THE STORM, Jane Donnelly
☐ 1859 THE MAN OUTSIDE, Jane Donnelly	☐ 1883 AUTUMN CONCERTO, Rebecca Stratton
☐ 1860 HIGH-COUNTRY WIFE, Gloria Bevan	☐ 1884 THE GOLD OF NOON, Essie Summers
☐ 1861 THE STAIRWAY TO ENCHANTMENT, Lucy Gillen	☐ 1885 PROUD CITADEL, Elizabeth Hoy
☐ 1862 CHATEAU IN PROVENCE, Rozella Lake	☐ 1886 TAKE ALL MY LOVES, Janice Gray
☐ 1863 McCABE'S KINGDOM, Margaret Way	☐ 1887 LOVE AND LUCY BROWN, Joyce Dingwell
☐ 1864 DEAR TYRANT, Margaret Malcolm	☐ 1888 THE BONDS OF MATRIMONY, Elizabeth Hunter
☐ 1865 STRANGER IN THE GLEN, Flora Kidd	☐ 1889 REEDS OF HONEY, Margaret Way
☐ 1866 THE GREATER HAPPINESS, Katrina Britt	☐ 1890 TELL ME MY FORTUNE, Mary Burchell
☐ 1867 FLAMINGO FLYING SOUTH, Joyce Dingwell	☐ 1891 SCORCHED WINGS, Elizabeth Ashton
☐ 1868 THE DREAM ON THE HILL, Lilian Peake	☐ 1892 THE HOUSE CALLED SAKURA, Katrina Britt
☐ 1869 THE HOUSE OF THE EAGLES, Elizabeth Ashton	☐ 1893 IF DREAMS CAME TRUE, Rozella Lake
☐ 1870 TO TRUST MY LOVE, Sandra Field	☐ 1894 QUICKSILVER SUMMER, Dorothy Cork
☐ 1871 THE BRAVE IN HEART, Mary Burchell	☐ 1895 GLEN OF SIGHS, Lucy Gillen
☐ 1872 CINNAMON HILL, Jan Andersen	☐ 1896 THE WIDE FIELDS OF HOME, Jane Arbor
☐ 1873 A PAVEMENT OF PEARL, Iris Danbury	☐ 1897 WESTHAMPTON ROYAL, Sheila Douglas
☐ 1874 DESIGN FOR DESTINY, Sue Peters	☐ 1898 FIREBIRD, Rebecca Stratton
☐ 1875 A PLUME OF DUST, Wynne May	☐ 1899 WINDS FROM THE SEA, Margaret Pargeter
☐ 1876 GATE OF THE GOLDEN GAZELLE, Dorothy Cork	☐ 1900 MOONRISE OVER THE MOUNTAINS, Lilian Peake
☐ 1877 MEANS TO AN END, Lucy Gillen	☐ 1901 THE BLUE JACARANDA, Elizabeth Hoy
☐ 1878 ISLE OF DREAMS, Elizabeth Dawson	☐ 1902 THE MAN AT THE HELM, Henrietta Reid
☐ 1879 DARK VIKING, Mary Wibberley	☐ 1903 COUNTRY OF THE VINE, Mary Wibberley
☐ 1880 SWEET SUNDOWN, Margaret Way	☐ 1904 THE CORNISH HEARTH, Isobel Chace

All books listed 75c

Harlequin Romances are available at your local bookseller, or through the Harlequin Reader Service, M.P.O. Box 707, Niagara Falls, N.Y. 14302; Canadian address: 649 Ontario St., Stratford, Ontario N5A 6W4.

Have you missed any of these . . .

Harlequin Presents..

All books listed are available at **95c each** at your local bookseller or through the Harlequin Reader Service.

Have you missed any of these . . .

Harlequin Presents..

All books listed 95c

Harlequin Presents novels are available at your local bookseller or through the Harlequin Reader Service, M.P.O. Box 707, Niagara Falls, N.Y. 14302; Canadian address: 649 Ontario St., Stratford, Ontario N5A 6W4.